NOT SO PRIVATE LIVES

(The follow-up novel of a short story entitled "Players at Play")

Copyright @ L Taylor 2018

ISBN 9798699315031

All characters are fictional.

Any similarity to any actual person is purely coincidental.

E & OE

Dedicated to- My husband John

Brief Encounter is a 1945 British romantic drama film directed by David Lean about British suburban life on the eve of World War 2, centering on Laura, a married woman with children, whose conventional life becomes increasingly complicated because of a chance meeting at a railway station with a married stranger, Alec. They fall in love, bringing about unexpected consequences.

  "The Rats"- An adulterous pair of lovers is asked, individually, to a London flat for drinks. The hosts are out of the country and the couple soon realize that they have been set up as victims. They are locked in and, in a flash, they are framed for murder.

NOT SO PRIVATE LIVES   L TAYLOR

The Drama Group

'But be not afraid of greatness: some are born great, some achieve greatness and some have greatness thrown upon 'em...

'No, no, no! *Thrust* upon them,' Ann interrupted.

'*Thrust upon them. Thy fates open their hands, let thy... let thy....*" continued Eric.

'*Let thy blood and spirit embrace them.*" Ann again butted in.

'Yes! Yes! Give me time to get it, for God's sake!' He snapped back at her.

'I was only...'

'I don't need a long feed. I know it! Give me time to get it back, woman! Give me time!'

Ann sighed heavily. Eric was 80 this year and she felt it really was time he took smaller roles in the Group's productions. She had worked with him now, on and off, for the last ten years. He had always been pedantic, stubborn and difficult. Egos were as fragile in these amateur productions as in the professional circuit of course and coming back to the group after her recent operation, had proved to her that there was more control to be had in the professional acting

NOT SO PRIVATE LIVES   L TAYLOR

world. They were paid after all, unlike this lot and thus more 'flexible'.

'You can't rehearse here! You must move downstairs!' Sheila appeared from behind the dusty curtain, thin and gaunt, her white hair further disheveled as she struggled to free herself from the curtain's hold.

'Sorry?' queried Ann.

'I said'… Sheila's voice was louder still.

'I KNOW what you said! Why on earth can't we rehearse here?'

'John wants it.'

'John wants what?' Ann queried again.

'John wants the room! We've only TWO weeks left, Ann and he wants the room! He'll have his workmate out and be sawing wood and banging nails and goodness knows what else…'

'Damn and blast!' Ann's voice, soft with an Irish lilt, held back her temper.

The doctor had warned her about keeping control of strong emotions like her anger. Blood pressure tablets could only do so much good.

NOT SO PRIVATE LIVES   L TAYLOR

'*Let thy blood…*' Eric began again, his skinny, veined arm raised above his head.

Ann looked from Sheila, at 78 to Eric 80. Both looked like walking skeletons. Both are dressed in white today; Eric in his Malvolio costume and Sheila in jumper and white polyester trousers. She suppressed a giggle and lowered Eric's arm with her chubby hand.

'We have to stop there, Eric.'

'But I've only just started. Don't you young'uns know anything about interrupting the flow…'

'John wants it.' Ann said.

John wants what?'

'Not that again!' Ann mumbled out loud.

'I need to do it again. Of course we must do it again. Rehearse! Rehearse! Rehearse! Always been my motto, Ann. 60 years at this game and it has always served me well.'

'The space is needed. John is making up scenery here today. We need to move to somewhere else, Eric.'

'Well, why didn't someone say? Why didn't John say? John who? Oh, yes, new chap. Plump! I remember him. He'd make a good Faust, he would. Can he act?'

'He makes the scenery Eric, that's all.'

'Oh. Then why are we letting him take over? We must rehearse, you know, Ann. We must rehearse! I've done this part THREE times in all during my career, or is it four...'

Eric stood gazing into space, trying to recall each production over the years. He mouthed figures and was now counting on the fingers of his left hand.

John, a red headed and red cheeked man in his fifties, pushed back the curtain and tied it back out of his way. He was carrying a black drill box and grinning broadly.

'We're just going, John. Eric! Eric!' Ann steered Eric back through the open space, down the wooden steps to the lower rooms.

Sheila followed behind them.

'Try not to make too much sawdust John, dear, there's a good lad!' Sheila said smiling, her loose dentures clicking as she did so.

NOT SO PRIVATE LIVES   L TAYLOR

John's face straightened and looked serious. He observed the pasty colour of Sheila's face and secretly wondered if the old girl was much longer for this world. She was a patient soul most of the time and generous in her home- baking. Those rock cakes of hers were lethal for his diabetes. She would be sadly missed, if her time had run out.

The converted barn had been the Amateur Theatrical's home for over 30 years now. The farmland behind it had changed quite drastically over those years and new houses now appeared as if overnight behind the barn. The local authority charged rent for the barn but also gave good subsidies towards the company's productions and membership fees helped pay towards other overhead costs like water rates and electricity.

Some of the members were as old but also proved as loyal as Eric and Sheila, thank goodness.

Descending the few wooden steps that led down from the level above, the three stood in the main room. To the left was a small kitchen and Ann headed there to put the kettle on and offer a comforting cup of tea. She hoped no one had inadvertently switched off the small refrigerator there otherwise the milk would be off again. Fortunately no one had.

NOT SO PRIVATE LIVES   L TAYLOR

Sheila followed behind her and took out a stained and rather rusty tray that she had brought back from Shanklin, Isle of Wight, too many years ago for her to care to remember, with three slightly chipped mugs and a small sugar basin. Eric had always been a devil for sugar in his tea, taking four spoons if he could get away with it. Not that you could ever see any weight gain on him. He had remained thin and wiry since Sheila had first met him coming out of a private boys' school when she was attending the Roman Catholic Girls' school that stood opposite. That was too many years, decades even, to want to mention. Funny though, how she could recall that day easier now than what she had planned to buy from the supermarket later today…

A drill could now be heard from the upper floor.

Eric was sitting at the long wooden table in the main room. Ann carried the tray and tea things to it and Sheila shuffled behind her with an old Peak Frean tin for biscuits which she regularly refilled.

Ann let the tea stew for a while and looked about her. Nothing had changed since her time away. The walls were covered with framed flyers of productions done over the years; some in black and white, some posters that were turning yellow with age and their corners torn where the drawing pins had come loose over time and been reinserted. The

NOT SO PRIVATE LIVES   L TAYLOR

book shelf in the corner still held old copies of Shakespeare and Oscar Wilde's plays and other volumes of more recent playwrights that sat awkwardly on top of rows, varied in sizes and some protruding.

She could see the dull and dusty silver cups on top and next to it the three rather crooked shelves that had been erected a long time ago to house the store of videos of the society's performances over the years.

There was now a small row of DVD's of their more recent productions.

A pile of folding chairs had been placed in the corner by the door and the settee and two armchairs that the wardrobe lady, Marcia had recovered had gained some new bright cushions. Sitting at the table was more comfortable for Ann, especially with her back problems. She knew that suite of old and how you sank into the failing upholstery and springs. It was hell trying to get back up out of it.

Eric strolled over to the fireplace to fetch a box of matches left there. The black iron guarded fireplace stood unattached, leaning against the bare brick wall of the barn, as a popular and often used prop.

'You're not going to light a pipe in here, Eric, surely!' Sheila warned him.

NOT SO PRIVATE LIVES   L TAYLOR

'Don't be a silly creature *all* your life, Sheila,' he replied dismissively and sat down, opened the box and started to build with the matches.

Sheila suddenly recalled how he had given up that filthy habit years and years ago. Why, even his mother was still active then. Funny how the memory played tricks on one...

'I had hoped to get through that act again, tonight. It's my favourite, you know. It's the funniest of Will's comedies. Tragic as well, of course. Did the wardrobe lady find the stockings for me to wear? I swear I left them here. I wouldn't have taken them home, like she suggested. Some people get the oddest ideas! I don't need keepsakes. What do I need keepsakes for? There's plenty of life in me yet- plenty still for me to do!' Eric declared.

Sheila doubted it but she knew better than to disagree with Eric.

'What time is the Committee Meeting tonight Ann? 7.30, was it?' She asked, changing the subject.

Ann looked at her watch. It was 7.10pm

'Yes. The others should start arriving soon.'

'I didn't make any cakes!' Sheila declared. 'I knew I had forgotten something I had to do today!'

NOT SO PRIVATE LIVES   L TAYLOR

The drilling upstairs had stopped as she was speaking.

'I hope he won't start again, whilst the Meeting is on.' Sheila said, gesticulating to the upper level and the handyman John with a nod of her head in that direction.

'I'll ask him to stop, if necessary,' said Ann, 'he's very obliging really. I don't know what we would have done without him on that Ayckbourn play.'

'He's too cocky, by half, if you ask me!' Eric's matchsticks collapsed as he spoke and he looked crossly at Sheila who had covered her mouth with her wrinkled old hand. He knew that gesture too. Stupid woman thought it funny!

The front door opened with an unexpectedly violent push.

Peter stood in the door way. He was the current Producer and was carrying his briefcase. Following him came Keith, the Treasurer, who was carrying a full supermarket carrier bag. Papers and files were sticking out of the top of it and the corners of the bags were looking worse for wear.

Peter was dark skinned with a full head of wavy dark hair. Wearing his tweed jacket and corduroy trousers on such a warm May evening he looked red in the

NOT SO PRIVATE LIVES   L TAYLOR

face and uncomfortable already. After they had all said their hellos in greeting, Ann took the tea pot back to the kettle in the kitchen and fetched some more mugs from the cupboard. None of the crockery matched now as pieces in sets had met the tiled floor too often and been replaced willy-nilly.

'Just waiting for Prue, then?' Keith observed and took out his red handkerchief to wipe the lenses of his spectacles. He was a short, balding man in his late 50's.

'We were trying to rehearse....' began Eric.

'Oh. Oh,' queried Peter, 'I thought we agreed John could have the upper floor for about an hour before the meeting began? Didn't he say he has some tables to finish, Eric?'

'Well if he did, no one told me!'

'I expect we all forgot,' suggested Sheila.

'I expect YOU forgot, Eric.' Ann snapped at him.

'I did **not** forget. I do not forget. I do not have a problem with my memory.' Eric stated angrily.

'Well, whatever. Shall we get on, get started then?' Peter opened his briefcase and took out some paperwork.

NOT SO PRIVATE LIVES   L TAYLOR

'Whose forgetting now, eh, Peter, eh? You just said we only needed Prue to start...' Eric chortled at his interjection.

'It was *me*! I said we had only Prue to wait for, Eric, not Peter.' Keith said, sitting forward and leaning on the carrier bag full of bills and accounts that he had placed in front of him on the table.

Ann poured two more cups of stewed tea and handed them to the new arrivals.

'Does it matter?' she exclaimed, 'WHO said WHAT?'

Fortunately the front door was then pushed open again and a draught of evening air, carrying the perfume of wallflowers from the garden over the fence, wafted in along with Prue.

'Am I late? I set out in good time...' she began.

Prue claimed to be the same age as Ann, mid- forties but few believed it. Unlike the dowdy, plump Ann, she dressed her tall, slender frame in diaphanous fabrics and boldly chose shades of green, or lilac or even fuchsia pink.

She also enjoyed wearing much dangling jewelry and the odd colour-matched scarf tied around her flowing greying hair. Ann had been known to

NOT SO PRIVATE LIVES   L TAYLOR

comment, when in a bad mood, that Prue certainly dressed the part of actress, if nothing else.

' I think we had bbbbbest get on then, folks...' said Peter, looking around the table at his fellow committee members. He handed out the agendas from his briefcase knowing full well that despite having emailed them copies, not one of them would have brought a printed copy with them....

*

"Thank goodness that's over, for another month!' said Prue as she climbed into her Ford Ka." Peter's stammer gets worse... lovely man, but limited as to what parts, if any, we can give him. But then he has put capital in, I gather."   Sheila was having a welcome lift home. She knew Trixie, her small and rather ancient terrier would be whining to go out for his last wee if she didn't get home fairly soon and the buses after 9.30pm were few and far between.

'Planning meetings do take some getting used to Prue, but are necessary. It seems we are all set for *"TWELFTH"*. I just hope Eric manages without TOO many prompts. He should give it up now at his age, he really should, whilst his reputation stands.'

'I'd like to meet the person brave enough to persuade him! Could it be you? You've known him for so long...' Prue suggested as she threw off her

NOT SO PRIVATE LIVES   L TAYLOR

shoes and drove in her bare feet. Sheila failed to even notice.

'I have dropped heavy enough hints but he glares back at me. Eric always was scary with his glares. And let's face it, we need some new, younger blood in the society and all the while we haven't got that, we are rather obliged to fall back on the old 'uns, myself included!' Sheila commented.

'I've taken flyers everywhere that I can think of. The corner shop has one, the Doctor's surgery, library of course…we'll just have to be patient and hope this latest campaign of Keith's works and some suitable people come forward,' Prue explained.

Sheila sighed heavily: 'I wonder if the company will even be running in five years' time! People have grown so lazy. So few even READ let alone are prepared to learn lines by heart!'

'Some truth in that but we mustn't despair, Sheila. My sister is talking to some of her drama pupils. She works at the local comprehensive- or Academy as they now call them, as you know, and she will try and enlist for us. It was good news about the local government subsidy- that should help the bank balance. Although, to be frank with you, Sheila, it seems healthy enough to me.'

NOT SO PRIVATE LIVES   L TAYLOR

'Oh, it is, never fear, with Keith in control! He's something of an Ebenezer! We're doing okay on that score. I wish he took more interest though at times, in the productions and less emphasis on cost…but there you go, we mustn't look a gift horse in the mouth, must we.

But we need to do something newer to get the bums on seats! Shakespeare is a once a year must of course, but Eric suggesting Dickens' " *Great Expectations*"… well, where are we to find a boy to play Pip?' Sheila asked rhetorically.

'When Eric said he had a pair of shorts and being of a small frame…. I nearly wet myself! He wasn't serious, surely?' Prue laughed out loud. It was a guttural, masculine laugh but infectious.

'Oh yes, he was. He'll do anything to get his own way. He was always the same. Living with his mother, never marrying, he was so spoilt, Prue. He doesn't know the meaning of real financial hardship, struggling to pay the rent and all the other necessities of life! And when *She* died he was left even more secure. Some people have all the luck in life! Here we are then.

Thanks again, Prue. See you at the Garden tomorrow. The forecast is good for open air!' Prue pulled up outside the block of flats and waited until

Sheila had climbed rather awkwardly from her passenger seat. They waved cheerily goodbye.

***

'Mike! I wasn't expecting to see you here tonight. We had your apologies!' exclaimed Ann. She had just washed up the last of the tea mugs and said goodbye to John the Job-man when Mike had so quietly entered the Barn. He was broad, stocky man, with dark beard and curly, jet black hair, of Italian ancestry.

'Yes, I know I did. It's because I had to see you.'

He stood behind her and his short but muscular arms encircled her waist as she stood at the kitchen sink. 'Not here, Mike. Not here!'

'No one can see, darling,' he whispered in her ear. She felt his beard brush her neck and could smell the cologne on his check shirt and waistcoat.

'If Geoff knew about us, it would kill him! It really would. I can't take any risks. Not since his bi- pass op.'

Mike pulled her around and kissed her fully on the mouth.

'You must stop!'

NOT SO PRIVATE LIVES   L TAYLOR

'I can't! I must have you again. After what we did that night upstairs in the store room…'

She giggled at this. 'Creasing all those lovely costumes. It's chocca up there. We should go through them and….

He stopped her mouth again with his. His large hands caressed her big round bottom and began to explore her.

'Everyone has gone. I waited behind the bushes! I saw John pull away in that estate of his.'

She pulled away from him and laughed again, the Irish twang of her voice noticeable now in the excitement of the moment.

'So you hid in the bushes? You hid like the naughty boy that you are!'

'I'll make you squeal with pleasure for that….'Mike said, grinning like a Cheshire cat.

Lowering her knees as he pulled her onto the kitchen floor, she could not resist him.

Geoff had made no sexual advances for months now and she so wanted sex…

NOT SO PRIVATE LIVES   L TAYLOR

The Secret is out

Eric stood mid stage, his white cotton nightshirt besmirched fittingly with dust and grime from his entrapment, as he gave his final lines.

"I'll be revenged on the whole pack of you!' he spat the words out into the audience.

Sheila sighed with relief. He had done it, finished the part with few noticed prompts. You had to give it to the ole fool… he COULD still do it…

Ann scrambled back stage where chaos ensued as the cast eagerly changed out of their costumes. The night had been humid and a storm was brewing. The audience had packed the deck chairs and stools and other seating had been fetched from the opera society's storeroom for the older in the audience to sit on. The younger ones readily gave up their seating and lay sprawled on the sun scorched lawns, enjoying their picnic hampers or carrier bags of foodstuffs; some swigging directly from their wine bottles others using plastic cups, which despite the warning notices, they would inevitably leave behind as discarded litter.

Ann, as director, had joined the cast at their last curtain call and made an awkward speech professing that although the play had given her much pleasure to direct, '*this bunch*' said as she was turning

NOT SO PRIVATE LIVES   L TAYLOR

towards the line of exhausted players to right and left of her, *' had been a nightmare!'*

 A noticeable hush had fallen over the audience at hearing this pronouncement and then some were heard to gasp.

Ann's husband, Geoff, housed in the shed at the top of the lawns where he operated the speakers, microphones and music centre, couldn't believe his wife's derogatory words.

What could have possessed the silly cow, he wondered? And why was that Mike person always sniffing around her like some dog on heat?

Despite the shade of the hut and the cool air from the small fan he had remembered to bring with him for that evening's final performance, Geoff's face grew redder at his wife's blatant criticism of her own cast. He was also sick and tired of being volunteered for the electrics and had threatened to retire from it for the last three years. This year he was determined would be his last.

John, scenery and props manager, was helping him out again tonight, lifting the heaviest gear away as he knew Geoff had been advised to take more care since his operation last year. John was a jovial chap and despite Geoff's finding little to be jovial about in life- what with Ann's financial demands on him and

NOT SO PRIVATE LIVES   L TAYLOR

his one and only daughter returning home with her young, noisy, three year old daughter, the father and her partner having deserted her- Geoff couldn't help but like John and smile at some of his jokes and antics.

"That wasn't a very nice comment about the cast, eh?" John remarked.

"Daft cow doesn't know what she is saying half the time. Her mouth has always been ahead of her addled brain!" Geoff responded." She may have passed exams and calls herself a qualified this and that... producer/ director... but she's put her foot right in it, tonight. And I overheard some of our actors swearing how they never would and never could work with her again! Some were threatening to leave before the final rehearsal because of all her bossiness! And so might I!"

John made no comment to this but took out his flask of tepid tea and offering Geoff a cup, which he refused, he thirstily finished the remainder.

If Geoff had overheard the squeals and panting noise of love- making that he had heard only the other night, emanating from the costume store, up on the upper level at the Barn, he would surely be madder still at his wife. And yet his own wife, Lin reckoned Geoff had a right to know about it before it all got out of hand. She reckoned if John told Geoff about it he might be able to step in and save his thirty year marriage with Ann.

Lin believed there must still be something worthwhile between the two after so many years together and that it could therefore be put right.

John now hesitated and swallowed hard. He should speak up and although it wasn't the best time, as Lin would say, whenever was? After they had cleared up and put everything back in the van, he and Geoff might not meet again for several months.

"Geoff, old chap… I need to tell you something…" he began nervously.

Geoff turned around and looked at the burly fellow. This was unheard of. John sounded uncharacteristically serious. He must stop and listen as John had often made his task that bit more bearable with his good humour. He deserved his ear if not any advice. Who was he to be able to advise anyone about anything anymore, Geoff thought gloomily.

"What is it, my old chum? What's up? If it's marital, I'm little use to you… but I can listen… I've learnt to listen being married to that Irish witch… she just prattles on and on… Sorry! I'll shut up and let you say what you have to…"

NOT SO PRIVATE LIVES   L TAYLOR

"Sit down on the garden bench here for a bit, Geoff. Did you want a smoke, at all?" John asked warily.

"Daren't now, you know…" Geoff said, pulling at his ear, a gesture John had often noticed when his companion was tired and stressed.

It was no good. It had to be said, so John continued.

"I was in the barn, doing some final nailing and sanding down. I could hear this couple…and they were… *at it*… they must have sneaked in and gone to lie amongst the coats and costumes up above me. I had been to the loo, see, and I guess they didn't realise I was still working that night on the scenery…"

"Oh yeah? Youngsters I bet." Geoff sniggered at the thought. "You should drop the latch behind you, you know, mate, every time… cos kids these days just want to do it and they don't care where…" Geoff's brow was creased and his cheeks flushed.

Bravely John continued. "I do always drop the latch. This couple had keys of course. And they weren't kids, Geoff… it was…"

"You saw them? What, *at it*? You dirty buggar!" Geoff laughed his rare and gruff little laugh that John had seldom heard before during their four years working together.

NOT SO PRIVATE LIVES   L TAYLOR

"I saw them leave together, Geoff, hand in hand…
and I saw the Ford Ka drive away…"

"A popular make, that model… good on petrol I
should imagine… "Geoff commented lightly and
then saw John's expression. He leant forward,
resting on his knees, then he sat back as if something
had finally hit him in the chest.

"Go on!" Geoff demanded.

"I'm sorry, Geoff… I am that sorry…" John, usually
never lost for words, now stumbled with them.

Geoff's expression changed. His lips were pale and
drawn back, his chin seemed to have jutted forward
and his eyes were piercing into John's.

"I said GO ON, f'ing hell, man, GO ON!"

"It's Ann… she and Mike…."

Geoff jumped up from the bench and despite his
weariness he marched from his companion, down
the side path that led to the front of the stage. One
speaker had been left standing, the last item to be
packed away. John still sat, horrified but unable to
think what he should do as he watched Geoff
reconnect the speaker.

Geoff raced back down the path to the hut, stepped inside and switched the speaker back on

His tirade began and was loud and clear.

"Come out of there, Mrs Director, Mrs Know-it-all, Mrs. Bloody bossy boots! Come out ANN, right now and face me!" he shouted out through the speaker.

A few stragglers from the audience turned towards the hut and looked bewildered. Could another play or announcement really be due at this late hour? Some had taken the side paths and were walking to their cars parked behind the shrubs.

From John's seat, he could see their heads and they too had stopped and were turning back.

Ann appeared front stage and was gazing in bewilderment towards the hut. Whatever was Geoff thinking of?

And so began their one and only fully public and publicised row. Their final row. The final act of their thirty year marriage? Mike came out on stage too to lend Ann support. He stood behind her and listened to Geoff's appalling language but said nothing.

Ann responded in just as loud and crude a choice of words, her voice growing shriller with anger as it carried on the stormy wind that was gathering

NOT SO PRIVATE LIVES   L TAYLOR

around them. Defending herself, declaring her love for Mike right there, in the full hearing of her remaining audience.

As the air grew bluer and thunder arrived, growling with them, Geoff and Ann's voices grew louder and madder, without any restraint, as if they were oblivious of anyone but the threesome.

Someone, within the cast or audience, must have used their mobile phone. When the police car arrived, seven minutes later, Geoff and Ann had finally stepped nearer and nearer each other and the wrestle had begun. Her fists flailing but missing every punch at her husband, Ann moved in even closer and tore at his receding hair. He pulled at her white shirt and tried to grab at her denim jeans as he shouted for her to show her best act of all to the waiting crowd. Her public coupling, he declared, would surely bring the house down!

The following weekend the local paper held a spread with the news of the best performance ever by this now even more popular, local am-dram society!

(End of short story first published in a trilogy of stories entitled "WHO PUT THE DOGS OUT? PLAYERS AT PLAY, FAT"

Now for the novel….

The Meeting

"So, what are we planning to do this time?" Sheila enquired as she opened her cake tin and began to display her home-baked cupcakes onto a doily covered plate stand.

"Oh, I think they're having a go at 'Brief Encounter.' Marcia replied as she took down the cups and saucers from the cupboard in the Barn's kitchenette.

"Great choice, it's one of Coward's finest productions. I think Peter plans to mix film version and play." Sheila commented.

"You know, this kitchen really could do with an overhaul." Marcia continued," it hasn't been touched in twenty years, I know."

"Don't be daft, Marcia, dear, that'll never happen. Look at your costume department…. It is overflowing and nothing done to help you-no new rails or hangers.

I don't know how you manage, I really don't. Most people would have given up by now…"

"I nearly did when I heard about…. you know… those two and what they had been up to…it's scandalous, if you ask me."

NOT SO PRIVATE LIVES   L TAYLOR

Nobody is, thought Sheila and nobody would try!
"You mean Ann and Mike… it's all been laid to rest apparently. She told me she'd finished it; couldn't leave her daughter and grandchildren to Geoff. Of course he's still like a bear with a sore bum. He'll probably never get over it or that scene last summer."

"I heard about it. Pity I was away in Spain, well, not pity… I mean to say I didn't actually witness it… but wasn't the affair blasted over the audience via the load speakers?"

"Indeed, it was dear. Pass me some spoons from the drawer, would you?"

"So, the daughter is still at their place and the child? Another marriage broken up; people just don't try hard enough to get on…. And then all this looseness about sex…" Marcia continued, filling the kettle with water from the tap which wobbled under her hand. "Just look at this! Who sees taps like this anymore? And the sink…. Well, I can't get rid of the stains… if the public saw this…"

 "Well, we must make sure they continue **not** to do so, dear, mustn't we."

The barn door opened with its usual creak as John, the handyman arrived.

NOT SO PRIVATE LIVES   L TAYLOR

"Do I smell my favourite brew?" he laughingly enquired.

"Oh, it's you, John. Yes, do sit down. Marcia has just got the pot to the kettle!" Sheila smiled fondly at him. He was a dear, rather naïve but so willing.

"Is anyone else on their way, I wonder? They all seem rather late this evening. Is there much traffic? I got an early bus. I can't drive any more, you see, with my condition- too shaky these days." Sheila explained.

"Hello there, John! Come to hammer and bang about?" Marcia suggested.

John frowned. "I can't make scenery or props without some noise and mess, Marcia. They want me to make a counter for the railway refreshment room for starters. And they're running a 60's short Christie play alongside it. I've only just found that out…." He placed his tool box and hold-all down beside one of the worn armchairs and then sat down at the table.

"Yes, they've never tried that before. That'll be a challenge for you. Still, after all that praise you got for the puppet theatre in the last Ayckbourn play I'm sure you will rise to the challenge." Marcia didn't look John in the eye as she made this comment.

In all her years with the society, no one had ever praised her for all her efforts.

John made no response. He took out a newspaper that he had brought with him, folded in his jacket pocket and laid it open to read so that he didn't lose his temper. Marcia was always sarcastic with him now since his success and mention in the local newspaper and the group's magazine. The green-eyed monster was a devil to fight against. He had met it often enough over the last three years as the Scenes and Props creator. He waited for the inevitable follow-up from her.

"Perhaps you might find some spare time to make a few rails for my costumes… I have the spare hangers… just lack of space as usual… but hangers would help." Marcia commented, noticing he was now reading his newspaper.

Fortunately, Ann and Keith the auditor and treasurer had now arrived as further distractions and he was not obliged to answer Marcia's repetitive request. Funny how she always chose to make some sarcastic comment that might sound like praise, but he knew was not meant so and then followed it up with the usual request for rails.

Seems some people never learnt, he decided, and it was invariably those would couldn't take no for an answer. As if he had time to make her damned rails with the work the Society expected of him.

Ann and Keith quietly sat down and took seats next to each other.

The door was flung open again as Prue arrived, her long hair straggling out of its clips and her full cotton skirt clinging damply to her lower legs. She was wearing a too short coat to cover her fully. Her silver bracelets jingled, as she bent down to pull the maroon skirt straight and stumbled into the sitting area of the Barn.

"Blasted weather, just you look at me! I look like the wreck of the… whatever that ship was!"

In unison the others replied "Hesperus!"

"This is a committee meeting isn't it? Should you still be here, John?"

John didn't even bother to look up at this further question from Marcia who had now placed the cake stand and displayed cupcakes in the centre of the table.

"John is *on* the committee, Marcia. I don't know how we could manage our budget without him and his savings." Keith answered her in his steady, gentle voice.

NOT SO PRIVATE LIVES   L TAYLOR

The sound of grit and pebbles being stirred by wheels of a fast car could be heard outside. Peter had drawn up in a silver Mercedes Benz recently bought to replace his Toyota but on its first outing to the A.B.T.S. meeting.

The barn door flew open once more. Peter stood in the doorway. He was wearing a baseball cap back to front on his head and his balding pate was well covered but for some stray side hair that now stood out like extra ears. No one spoke. He took off his dripping wet nylon sou'wester to reveal a denim jacket covered in badges.

There was a muffled snigger from the members of the cast and John boldly greeted their producer with the cheeky words "Howdy, partner! Come and join us, buddy! Where's the helmet and boots?" This brought out hoots of laughter from the others.

Peter glared and motioned towards the table.

"Put it there!" said John, holding out his hand in greeting and still giggling. Peter ignored the gesture and pulling out his wooden seat, dragged it noisily across the wooden flooring, removed his baseball cap, sat himself down and said nothing. Keith, who was sitting next to John, knocked his calf with his shoe under the table as a warning to stop teasing him.

NOT SO PRIVATE LIVES   L TAYLOR

"Cake?" offered Sheila.

"Oh, they look nnn… nice but I am still on a strict diet, Sheila." Peter responded, shuffling with his shoulder bag, his colour raised with chagrin.

"Let's get on!! Ann suddenly spoke her first words. "I haven't got all day, even if you lot have! I've a daughter and grandchild to feed when I get home…"

At attention, at this, her usual commanding tone, the cast automatically sat back in their seats. "No Geoff?" Prue asked, pulling up the sleeves of her brightly patterned cardigan. Ann glowered at her possible inference.

"I mean… is Geoff not coming too?" Prue wriggled in her seat in discomfort. *Oh, why did she always manage to put her foot in it?*

"Why should he? He's lighting, isn't he?" Ann abruptly replied.

"And speakers…" *Prue could have bitten off her tongue. She had done it again*!

"Yes... AND SPEAKERS! Now for goodness sake, Keith, give us the figures do!" Ann's hand shook as she took up her cup of tea and sipped at it.

"We're fine. 14 thou still banked and the last play… well, being in the church hall, it didn't make much but enough to cover costs." Keith reported, handing out copies of the accounts around the table.

"People hate that church hall. I DO so wish we didn't have to use it, even though I realise how cheap it is to hire." Sheila commented.

"Moving on…" motioned Ann. She turned to John. "Is the scenery going to be costly, John? How on earth are you going to tackle two different timescales?"

"I have it in hand, Ann. I've brought a rough drawing for you and made it as simple as I could." Much to Sheila's sudden look of horror, fearful for her baking pride and joy, he shoved the cake stand from the middle of the table and spread open a large sheet of A3 paper; those who could not see it, soon rose and gathered around to hear how John would tackle the task.

"The chief idea is that these walls hang over the others… the scenery of one play can fit over the stationary scenery of t'other… and all we have to do is lift off the relevant scenery to reveal whichever play we are about to perform…"

"Why, that's brilliant!" Keith commented.

NOT SO PRIVATE LIVES   L TAYLOR

"It certainly looks good…" Peter couldn't help responding.

"It would be too heavy to lift up and down… and wood is so expensive…" Marcia began.

John's bushy red eyebrows lifted upwards at this criticism. "We won't be asking **you** to lift it, Marcia. We men will do that easily. And I am reusing wood from previous sets."

"Whose mad idea was it to do two different period plays anyway?" Sheila enquired. The rest of the cast turned their attention towards Peter.

John stepped in. "Don't you worry, Peter, old chap… it'll work fine. I could have done with more notice… but I'm used to that with you am-drammers! It's novel and should pull in the punters, don't you think so?" he asked, turning now towards Keith.

Peter managed a small smile of gratitude.

"Too right, John. All we need now is to cast… who's doing what part and then we can call it a night, I guess. Where's Eric these days? He surely isn't still going to want a part?" Ann said.

"Don't bank on that, Eric will want to be on that stage until he drops on that stage, if I know him. And if anyone here does, it's surely me." Sheila stated.

Sighs were heard all round and there were nods of agreement.

"Well, his absence means we will finish early…. That much is sure!" Sheila poured herself another cup of tea and the cast set about diarising dates for auditions and suggested casting for their regular players.

The two new plays were to be performed at the local Pavilion in just two months' time….

"A wandering minstrel I, a thing of shreds and patches… dee dum dee dee dee…and dreamy lullaby! AND DREAMY LULLABY!"

Eric sang louder as he dusted around his small cottage; banisters, hall shelves with plants, door frames… mustn't forget door frames.

"I've still got it! Oh, yes, you lot! No doubt sitting round that committee table, sipping free tea and cakes… you won't get rid of me in a hurry, no siree!"

He stopped, feeling breathless, and sat on the bottom of the stairs. Looking around for any missed dust or cobwebs, he thought about those last days when Mama had finally passed on. Poor soul, 98 years old, bed ridden at the end. Upstairs in that larger of the two bedrooms was where it had happened.

The doctor had just been to attend to her and the nurse was late coming… He hadn't been able to vacate the smaller and take her room. Too many sad memories. And then there was that shadow, the shadow that always appeared beside her old mahogany wardrobe. He hadn't emptied that either nor opened its door. It would smell and what if… what if something lurked… he shivered and shakily stood up from the stairs, holding the wooden newel knob tightly with cold, bony hands. Best make a cup of tea and think of something else. Sheila of course, Sheila might come to visit and he could broach the subject of clearing Mama's old clothes… some Edwardian dresses would perhaps be useful for Marcia's wardrobe.

The telephone rang. Eric put down his flowery china cup on the saucer and slowly got up to answer the old dial phone.

"Why shouldn't I? I didn't say I was free today, anyway." He replied to the voice at the other end of the line.

"I'll get a copy of the minutes. You always ramble on about nothing anyway…

Who, who did you say is the real rambler? What did you say, Sheila, eh? Eh? Listen, I'm busy.

Yes, yes, I shall be there for the auditions. I was thinking, isn't it time we did a Gilbert & Sullivan? They always go down well. What? Too old-fashioned? Nonsense! Why, half our trustees are our age, dear. You really must wake up your ideas, woman. Sheila? Sheila, are you there? I wanted to ask…" Eric replaced the receiver. Silly woman had cut herself off again. She was always doing so these days. He wasn't going to ring back, spending unnecessary money to listen to her yacking on! Pity he hadn't got the time to ask her about those clothes though; she could be the one to open that ghastly wardrobe. She was all mouth most of the time, so she could do it… Still, there was the auditions evening to look forward to… now where should he write that date down???

Ann arrives home

Ann parked her 4 x 4 in the driveway of her 30's style semi-detached house.

Kept brief by Eric's absence, thank goodness the meeting was over. "It's only me!" She called out as she clip-clopped with her kitten heels across the black and white tiled hallway. She gazed ahead towards the modern extended kitchen and could see the back of Geoff standing by the work-station, chopping some vegetables. He must surely have heard her calling; her voice was renowned for its carriage. Still, he made no answer. Still sulking no doubt and still she was not forgiven for her fling with Mike. It had just been some fun for once. Would he ever be able to forgive and forget? What was it Pope had said- *To err is human, to forgive divine?*" Her husband certainly had no divinity in him. Mummy had always been against her marriage to Geoff; declaring he was the wrong class of person for her. Perhaps she was right all along. Mothers knew their daughters best.

"Chopping carrots, I see? Casserole tonight, isn't that what we said?" She slipped her arms around Geoff's waist affectionately but there was yet again no response. She desisted and walked towards the wine rack and pulled out a new bottle of claret.

"That dippy girl we call our daughter, can't even chop carrots properly. She left them in chunks instead of dicing them properly. I've had to re-do all the veg. Why you didn't take more time teaching her to cook, I don't know…she's spoilt rotten, Ann." Geoff stated and with the edge of his knife, pushed the said carrots into the casserole dish with the rest of the vegetables and meat.

"They're only young once, Geoff, dear. Life has enough burdens for us all to carry" she responded, pouring out a large glass of wine and taking a large sip.

He turned around towards her, having heard the glug of the wine as it hit the bottom of the wine glass, "Yes, but she's 26 now and has a child and as for burdens… I don't need to carry her and hers for the rest of my years." Anne didn't respond to his criticism. The wine would ease her annoyance at his aggravating endless criticism of her parenting. She had always hoped their only child would marry well and have a cook to do such chores for her but she had got herself pregnant and then under her father's stern reaction, the young couple had been persuaded to marry.

"Isn't that a rather large glass? What did the doctor say about your blood pressure and your diabetes? He asked, sternly.

"Sod the doctor! I haven't had a good day and then I had the meeting… goodness knows who will turn up for casting those two plays."

"Did Eric turn up then?" Geoff was wiping his hands on the kitchen towel and removing an apron. Ann lifted the bottle to indicate his joining her but he nodded his head in the negative; his ulcer was cured and he wanted it to stay that way. It had been such a painful time.

"No, that was the only consolation. Peter and his mad ideas. You should have seen what he turned up in this evening! We all couldn't contain ourselves and chuckled away. Denim jacket with buttons and a baseball cap. I don't usually like John's comments, but this evening he hit the nail on the head…"

"Hahaha!" Geoff now actually laughed. "I bet he did. Knowing our John! What was that all about then?"

"Probably his daughter Rachel is behind it. Telling Daddy to get 'with it' or some such nonsense. He's exchanged his Toyota for a Mercedes Benz… silver coloured."

"No way! He must be mad at his time of life. I bet John had something to say about that too… he's well up on cars and mechanics.

"Which reminds me, you will be okay to help with the lighting and so on again this time round? Ann asked, having now drained her glass.

"Yes. John's doing the stage fittings and props."

"Of course. We can't easily find anyone else." Ann moved across to the casserole dish and placed it in the heated oven and turned on the timer.

"There's nowt wrong with him, Ann. Just because he's been a good friend. A good friend tells you those things you might not want to hear…"

At these words, Ann knocked her glass against the tap in an attempt to rinse it. The glass shattered and she had cut her hand.

Geoff immediately went to her assistance and placed her hand under a running tap. "It'll be okay" he said, taking it into his large hands and wiping hers dry.

"It isn't a deep cut. No hospital job. Clumsy old thing, you!"

Ann looking into his deep brown eyes. "Yes," she replied, "Clumsy. Sorry."

He was just about to say something more, when their daughter, Susie came into the kitchen.

NOT SO PRIVATE LIVES   L TAYLOR

"Oh, Mummy, I'm famished. When will we be eating?"

Geoff began to load some dishes into the dish washer and just sighed heavily out loud.

Ann's Comeuppance.

Geoff, with John's help, had been busy checking and rewiring some of the speakers, sorting the missing and damaged bulbs for the lighting for the two plays. John had shown him how the double scenery would work and he was most impressed. But he went home feeling very tired.

Entering the kitchen, he noticed that Susie had still not loaded the dish waster nor attempted to tidy up. Ann had been busy baking scones and cakes for the staff after their first casting meeting tomorrow and was taking a bath upstairs.

Susie waltzed into the kitchen and took a bar stool. She started to read a woman's magazine.

"You were asked to clear up, young lady. Where's the child?" Her father enquired sternly.

"With her other grandma." She replied, taking out a cigarette and matches to light it.

"You know your mother won't have smoking indoors, I'm not allowed the odd one indoors and neither are you." He told her crossly.

Susie had not lost the fat from her childbirth, which was two years since. She was sitting engrossed in her magazine, wearing a pair of denim dungarees

NOT SO PRIVATE LIVES   L TAYLOR

over a much stained tee shirt. She had not washed her hair, which like Ann's was naturally rather wavy and frizzy. She wore it longer and it hung greasily against her neck and shoulders. Her face was full and round, with some freckles which he could recall Ann once had when he had first courted her, all those years ago.

"Don't be silly Dad. Mummy won't mind *me* smoking."

"You mean, she lets you...?"

Emboldened, she continued to take out her lighter from the pocket of her dungarees. "Of course she does. Daddy, you should know your place!" and laughed. That was it. Geoff left the sink and the washing up and grabbed her cigarette from her mouth.

"Go and pack! Go back to your husband. Leave your brat with their Grandma and get out of my sight!"

"But Daddy... Mummy wants me to stay!" Susie was shocked at his harsh grip of her shoulders. He meant business and suddenly she was rather afraid of him.

 Geoff's colour had risen with rage. He stepped over to the telephone on the wall and dialed for a taxi.

NOT SO PRIVATE LIVES   L TAYLOR

"What are you thinking of, Daddy dearest…Mummy will be so cross with you..." She said, trying to placate him. Who knew what he might do next?

Geoff now fetched Susie's anorak from the hall and tossed it to her.

"Put it on!" he demanded, taking some bank notes out of his wallet and handing them to her." "Go back to your husband, the man you married. If he has any sense left, he'll be there waiting and ready for you!"

Susie stood shocked and amazed at this change in him. She hurriedly put on the coat.

Geoff pushed her to the front door and then outside, on to the pavement. She heard him dropping the door latch behind her. Susie called through the letter box. "The taxi is here. You'll regret this when Mummy finds out!" It was all she could find to say in protest. She felt quite shattered at this type of behaviour from her father. What had come over him? Still, Mummy would come downstairs and sort it and probably would call her at the flat and tell her to of course come back…

Geoff heard the taxi pull up over the gravel and pull away. He peered through the net curtain at the front bay window and saw that his daughter had actually gone. So, it paid off to be so assertive. Just wait until Ann came down.

NOT SO PRIVATE LIVES   L TAYLOR

Geoff smoked two cigarettes. He wasn't supposed to smoke any of course.

He climbed the stairs. It was just 3pm in the afternoon but he was ready for action.

Ann floated into the double bedroom, dressed in only her dressing gown after a long soak in the bath.

She sat at her dressing table and combed the ends of her curly dark hair. He noted how it was greying in places but it was rather more attractive to his eyes.

"What was all that noise downstairs? Did I hear a car?"

"Yes. I've sent our daughter home to her husband. I'll pack her things later and send them on. Our grandchild is with Alan's parents for now." He stated in a matter of fact tone.

"You've done what? She can't go back to that…. that ape of a husband! She needs our help through this difficult separation." Ann said, her voice anxious and loud.

"Ape is he? In what way, dear Ann?" Geoff sat on the end of the bed and watched her cleanse her face with some cream. She had taken the rest of the day off from her managerial position within the local government office. She had worked there long enough to take time when she chose.

"Well, he was never good enough for her…"she tried to explain.

"Like me, you mean? She married him. There must have been something between them." He commented, watching her as she sat preening herself.

Her legs were still good and she had lost a stone or more since her diagnosis of diabetes.

"She deserves better." Ann claimed.

"I spoke to Alan the other day. We agreed about what she, and you, deserve."

"Listen, Geoff, I know we have had a rough time… but really, you can't just let her go back…" she swiveled her chair around to face him.

"It's time she stood on her own feet and took the consequences of her actions, Ann. I love her as much as you do, you know. What is it about being alone with me? Is that the reason you hold on to her so tightly? You aren't doing her any favours."

Ann's voice quivered. "I, I, don't know what you mean?"

NOT SO PRIVATE LIVES   L TAYLOR

"An empty nest, however big or small, means a couple have time to get to know each other again. Can't we try that? I know my heart op meant … well, less intimacy between us…" he began to try and explain.

"But that's exactly it, you see. The consultant explained it was good for the heart… sex, I mean… but you just shut down on me!" There were tears in her eyes.

"Nan," he stood up and moved towards her, sitting still at her dressing table. He knelt down beside her and took her hands in his. He had not called her Nan for some time, a sure term of endearment.

"Oh, goodness me, Geoff. When you're tender like this…" she spoke softly.

He saw her robe had fallen open, revealing her still slender thighs and the wisp of pubic hair at the top of them. He began to stroke her legs with his big, warm hands. Ann's eyes pleaded.

"Come over here then… and we'll try again…" Geoff pulled her upright and led her over to their bed. "Now we are alone… just us two… no more child to shield and no need to hide behind her…"

Audition Time

The lights were working well and John and Peter had rehearsed the change of scenery. It had been decided that once the first play had been performed and then the second play's scenery attached and performed, that this final scenery would the first play on next time and so on… it would add variety and save some time and effort.

Some of the applicants were known, experienced players who performed across the county in other Am Dram Societies and had varying skills; some could sing, dance and play an instrument as well as act a role. These people could therefore afford to be choosy. The few young people who attended were invariably still at drama school or good at drama at their local grammar or comprehensive. Most were keen to see what roles were on offer and how much dialogue they would need to learn.

Bow ties and suits went unnoticed or merely raised a giggle or two from the younger ones.

Geoff had been whistling. John had never seen him so happy. All he would say was that he and Ann had sorted out their differences. John was pleased for him and had no wish to pry.

Ann kept finding an excuse to slip backstage to see Geoff and when she clutched his hand and smiled up at her husband, John knew it was time to take a tea break. They were like honeymooners and he was not alone in noticing the change in them. The rest of the players whispered the news that Susie, their daughter, had finally gone back to her husband and surmised that this could be the cure for Geoff and Ann's ailing marriage.

No one mentioned Mike. No one now bothered to make any snide remarks to either of the couple. However, other problems with other people continued to brew…

"How are you, Eric? I tried to ring you at home the other week when you didn't turn up for the Committee Meeting but I got no reply." Sheila opened the Barn door to allow him in.

He was dressed in his suit, a satin grey waistcoat, with a clean, striped shirt and red spotted bow tie. Eric felt sure that the first thing applicants would take note of was the good impression smart dress gave from the very beginning.

"I was probably otherwise engaged." Eric replied. ! Ah! Yes!" He remembered his plan now to clear his late mother's wardrobe. "I want you to come to tea, Sheila… you can bring some of your home-made cakes if you wish… come sometime fairly soon, I have a little job you might enjoy…"

"Really?" Sheila responded, cautiously, "Not another dirty task in the garden, I trust?"

"What *can* you mean?" he snapped back.

"Last job you claimed I *'might enjoy'* was pulling up that deep-rooted forsythia bush, if I recall." She left him sitting in his favourite armchair, positioned in the corner by the wooden stairs that led up to the upper floors, and went to help with the teas. He would always claim this high-backed chair as his; Marcia had been persuaded to re-cover it recently in a green velvet material and he could lean his skinny arms on the rigid wooden arms; he seemed to fit into it like a glove. From this position he had a clear view of the entire main room and right into the kitchenette and through the window to watch who would be next to arrive and who was late. He had opined on many an occasion that lateness didn't set prospective players a good example either but people would still arrive late.

 Eric, Peter, Sheila, Ann and Geoff, Prue, Marcia and Keith flowed in randomly to meet the applicants for the two plays they intended showing later that spring- namely "Brief Encounter" and a lesser known but one act murder/thriller by Agatha Christie's "The Rats."

"Ah!" exclaimed Eric as the last of them arrived and took one of the odd seats that were placed against the wall, some used in staging, others left to gather dust." So, may we begin?"

"I think the interviewees are up above you, Eric, with Marcia. She's casting a quick look over the build of them, in case her wardrobe can't match their sizes near enough to make alterations!" Prue explained, straightening her skirts and retying one of her boot laces.

It looked as if she had hurriedly her face make-up as her lipstick was smudged and one eye held no mascara. "Drat!" she mumbled, holding a broken lace in her hand.

"Why are they up there? We haven't selected yet!" Eric asked tetchily.

Ann overheard his criticism and leant forward in her chair. She spoke quietly. "We haven't got that many applicants, Eric… we cannot be too choosey… seeing the costumes on offer often encourages people… gets them interested…"

"Humph!" was his response. "I'm always available. I can do more than prompts, you know!" Ann made no reply. Confidentially, the group had all agreed that Eric could not be relied on anymore to learn his lines thoroughly without strange ad-libbing. Nor did he seem able to accept stage directions without making criticisms.

As they returned to the lower floor, Peter stood up and welcomed the applicants, offering them what seats they could find vacant. "Come on in! Do come on in"! There was a spare pouffe, which young Carey, Mike's actor son, soon took, and a basket chair and two stools were also soon taken up at his welcome.

Peter was dressed more soberly this evening, wearing a favourite green sweater over a polo shirt and corduroy trousers that were a rather dubious sandy colour.

The actor, Ian stood over six feet tall, was clean shaven and wore his snowy white hair short. He had a rather too large nose for his long face but he had been selected for several non-speaking parts on television dramas and was also a much liked actor with the Am- Dram sect. Reliable, non- critical, quietly spoken, he had managed, with his wife's support, to make a living out of acting. So, as he was available, he was the first choice for the main role of

Dr Alec Harvey and didn't hesitate to accept it nor the cup of tea and sandwich offered from Sheila's large serving plate. Ann had prepared these, Sheila noted, and not entirely cut off all the crusts as she would have made sure to do.

"Carey, do help yourself. Good to see you here. Pity about your father... I mean, his not acting with us anymore... is he busy? Directing perhaps?" Eric mischievously enquired.

Carey's cheeks coloured. "He's working in Nottingham at present, Eric. Very happy there. Some musical, I believe."

"Good for him!" Stated Keith in a loud voice and casting a quick look towards Ann and Geoff, who seemingly had not overheard Eric's question, noted that they were still sitting together on the couch.

"I have copies with me, on loan... Samuel French as usual..."he quickly handed out the dozen booklets. Geoff took Ann's hand in his and gave it a quick squeeze. Feeling self-conscious, she stretched her legs out in front of her and gazed at her own tights

Young Carey, Mike's only son, happily took the part of Bert Godby the station porter of Milford Junction, confidently stating how he had played older men before with some success.

"So, who's playing the main part of Laura Jesson - the married woman tempted into adultery by Dr Alec?" enquired Prue, averting her eyes from Ann by playing with the silver bangles on her wrists.

Peter, director and producer of the play, quickly responded." Ann has asked for that demanding rrr....role and I feel sure she will do it justice." He put on his bravest smile for them all, turning his head so that everyone present could witness his pleasure at this announcement.

"Now, there's a surprise! Yes, experience always shows!" Eric commented.

"What *exactly* are you trying to say, Eric? Let's face it, you always have something to say but don't always make yourself too clear, these days, old chap!" Geoff spoke loudly and took Anne's hand in his again, a gesture not missed by the rest of the company.

"Oh, nothing we aren't *all* thinking, I'm sure…. How good she will be, how well suited to it- Laura has children too, doesn't she?" He sat back in his armchair, totally relaxed, his arms lying casually on the sides.

"Prue, I think you would make a lovely job of the snooty lady behind the counter in the Refreshments Room…now, what was her name?" Peter flipped through his copy of the play.

"Oh, you mean Mrs Baggot, who Albert Godby flirts with all the time? Yes, Carey and I will enjoy that one. It is all set in the Refreshments Room … is John about?"

"She acts all posh too, puts on such a refined voice, you'll enjoy that you know, Prue.' Sheila began. '*I don't know to what you are referring*' is one of her lines.

Their flirtation is in contrast to the main characters' *real* love of course…" Sheila continued and then, feeling uncomfortable and wishing she had not explained as much, she suddenly shut up.

Prue glowered at her. "I could have done the main role. Ann and I are of the same age…." She commented, gazing over to Peter.

"Ann is playing it, Prue, dear and that is final." Peter told her.

NOT SO PRIVATE LIVES   L TAYLOR

Still annoyed at the choice, Prue huffed and fidgeted back in her chair.

"The part of Dolly will be taken by Sheila. She's a bit part at the end, so Sheila can still act as prompt. Okay with that, Sheila?"

Yes, of course... I've played it before you know..."

"Sorry?" Peter sounded confused.

"Yes, I played the main character, Laura... there are some wonderful scenes... where she is looking at camera in the film, but at the audience in the play. " *This misery can't last, not even life lasts very long"* she says it so sadly and towards the end, on parting from Alec, ""*I want to die. If only I could die"* Some actual tears appeared at the corners of Sheila's eyes.

"Isn't that the bit in the film with Celia Johnson where she runs out onto the station as if she wants to jump on the line and kill herself?" Marcia queried.

"Moving on, then..." Peter swiftly interrupted. "Our John has got some recorded steam train sounds for background and I shall be operating the sound system. Geoff is doing lights, sss...speakers and giving some much needed and appreciated help with the scene changes, yes?" He turned to Geoff who merely nodded in the affirmative and looked thoughtful at the mention of suicide.

NOT SO PRIVATE LIVES   L TAYLOR

"Yes, it *is* set in the Refreshments Room only and John has something special to show us later on." Peter informed them all.

"He's a clever chap!" Keith stated loyally,

"He certainly is. 'The Rats' play, which we will look at in two days' time, is a short one act and the usual murder. Carey is taking another part in that and Richard, who some of us know, is taking the other main male part. My daughter Rachel and her friend Evie are new to it but are going to play their partners. We have fresh young bloods after all! It's a clever 60's adaptation re scenery, thanks to John.

The counter turns upside as a coffee table and Marcia is painting us a large mural of skyscrapers, some city life as background. Oh, if anyone can find an old, antique looking knife for the murder weapon, I would be grateful." Peter asked of anyone of them listening. However, he was met with no response.

At this juncture, John was heard coming down the steps from the upper level where he had been assembling a cardboard object. He was wearing his paint splattered overalls.

"Do take a cuppa, John and a seat. There's some cake over, I think… come and join us." Peter said welcoming him.

NOT SO PRIVATE LIVES   L TAYLOR

John stood grinning, one arm behind his back.

"In a minute, I need to get out of these dusty things before I sit down proper!"

Then he took out the surprise held hidden behind his large frame. Two of the young newcomers quickly came forward to see what he held.

Sheila hastened across the floor with them. "Goodness me!' she gasped as she looked. "It looks so real... but surely, it can't be..." John held out for inspection a cardboard replica of an old fashioned till, with pound signs on keys and a drawer beneath.

The rest of the company, except Eric who was blowing his nose in his handkerchief as a gesture of disinterest, now also came over to view John's latest creation.

"Marvellous!" claimed Peter.

"You're a clever buggar!" Geoff said, tapping John on the shoulder.

Eric's voice was clearly heard from his corner seat. "It won't ring though... you forgot that, didn't you. Those old tills had a bell when you pressed the drawer for change etc.... I remember them of course and more accurately." He said, sneering at John.

John grinned some more. "Problem solved, Eric. Out of sight of the audience and on the counter, we place a hand bell, one discovered up in the loft here, and the actor merely has to press it as they handle any cash or coins from the extras, those few customers who appear briefly at the counter, and no one will know any different! We even have some pre decimal coinage to use!"

Eric sniffed disdainfully.

"What's "Rats" all about then?' Eric asked." It isn't one I'm familiar with so it can't have been her best!" he suggested.

"The usual eternal tangle of lovers leading to a murder." Carey explained. "Actually I think it's a good choice of contrast to… "Brief Encounter," he went on to explain further, "Because the couple in love don't succumb… whereas in RATS…which is set two decades later, with morals fading, and little romance, they certainly have!

There are just four players… the main character pushed her husband off a cliff and is now having an affair with this David. They get set up by her late husband's friend… with her second husband's body hidden in an old chest and only their fingerprints on the murder weapon. It's a clever plot and complete in the one act! They get locked in this high-rise

NOT SO PRIVATE LIVES   L TAYLOR

flat… trapped like rats which they prove to be. No love there, just sex."

There had been total silence at Carey's full explanation of the plot.

"Ah, it's about fornication, betrayal, deception and lies! How common all that now is!" Eric quipped. Still no one spoke.

Leaving the group to admire his work, John now struggled out of his overalls to reveal his clean jeans and tee shirt beneath. He took the last of the sandwiches and a cold orange drink from the jug and seated himself down by the table.

Sheila sat beside him. "Did you hear that I once played that main part in 'Brief Encounter?'" she asked.

Geoff and Ann were standing beside them, pouring the last of tea from the teapot.

"It might be a bit over-brewed now, darling," Ann warned her husband.

Gazing down at his wife, Geoff smiled warmly at her.

"The best bit of the play is its ending." He said, not taking his eyes off her, "when her husband says, and

NOT SO PRIVATE LIVES   L TAYLOR

I think Peter is having it played as an offside voice, *"You've been a long way away. Thank you for coming back to* me*."* Ann and Geoff gazed into each other's eyes.

Sheila felt a warm glow of pleasure at sight of them, together again. "Oh, yes, surely…. That final line is enough to make me cry, every time"…she commented.

When the group finally broke up and departed for their homes, Sheila gave both Ann and Geoff extra big hugs in farewell.

First Night

The first performed play, "BRIEF ENCOUNTER" certainly went down well. Unfortunately, "THE RATS" play that followed that first night, was a little known one and not classed as one of Agatha Christie's better plays. It didn't help that the younger members of the cast needed so many prompts in sharp contrast to the earlier play.

Ann shone; at the end of the play, a chair was placed far right, and the curtain lowered half way. There Ann sat, staring out at the audience. Then a voice, presumed to be her husband's, spoke the famous last line…. *"You have been so far away. Thank you for coming back to me."* The words had been recorded by Marcia's husband and beautifully spoken but it was Ann's expression, as she sat there gazing into space yet towards her audience, that raised such emotion and brought the house 'down' with such applause at her performance that night.

 She repeated it on the nights that followed and was met with the same appreciative applause in response. The rest of the cast agreed she had never played a part so well, so convincingly. They muttered how they had not realised the untapped talent that lay within her.

NOT SO PRIVATE LIVES   L TAYLOR

Geoff watched her closely as he lowered the lights for that last scene. What was he to make of her these days? She had always been passionate, bossy, and dominant as far as he would allow… it was down to her Irish blood surely and now, despite their renewed intimacy, he still had these doubts that niggled as they stirred within him. Did that look of hers stem from loving Mike still? Was it really just an affair that was now over, as she had claimed? Would he ever know? Should he let it go….?

As Geoff and John sat drinking squash after moving the scenery around, Geoff found himself confiding more in John. He seemed so easy to talk to.

"She's always been passionate... I mean, our relationship has always been very physical, despite the passing years. We shout and bellow at each other as if we hate one another, and at times I guess we do… as unfortunately was witnessed only too recently, and in public. But then we make it up… you know what I mean?"

John just nodded and let him continue talking.

"She seems different somehow. That last scene, even in rehearsal it bothered me and now live, she seems even stronger. Listen to the applause! And now an ovation? Unheard of! Does she still love him? The

NOT SO PRIVATE LIVES   L TAYLOR

question haunts me despite everything… I wish it didn't!"

"Listen, mate." John began, putting down his cheese sandwich pack brought from home and made by his loving wife, Lin, "maybe she does, maybe she doesn't… but what matters is that she has chosen to stay with you, to come back to you, like the line says…. Enjoy it, don't spoil it for her or yourself…"

"But that's just a play…"

"Lin always says that art reflects life…" John responded, hoping he could lessen some of Geoff's doubts, only too aware that he had already undergone surgery for his heart and extra stress could never be good for him.

"Yes, you could be right." Geoff sighed heavily. "But does she love me, that's the question. Really love me like I do her?"

"I guess you can love more than one person … but she's made the choice and that was you." *Would he ever be persuaded, John wondered.*

"I need a fag"….

"You know you shouldn't, Geoff! But go on… only a few drags then…"

NOT SO PRIVATE LIVES   L TAYLOR

Disaster Strikes.

"Oh, Nnnoo! Oh, NO!"…. Peter pressed his mobile phone to off and sat down in Eric's chair by mistake. He held his head in his hands and swayed his body from side to side like a very upset child.

"What on earth…?" Sheila began, tea towel in hand from out of the Barn's kitchenette. They had met to try and find more suitable costumes for the second play, THE RATS, hoping a more period wardrobe might prompt a better performance and audience reaction. Richard was wonderful in his part but the younger actors had forgotten paragraph after paragraph of script and poor young Carey had to step in and ad-lib to get the scene moved on in an attempt to make any sense of it to the audience."

It had been a nightmare. Now what? She wondered. Thank goodness "BRIEF ENCOUNTER" had replaced it as the second play which meant the audience would go out the door fully satisfied with that one and hopefully dismissing the previous disastrous play. It certainly overshadowed it in every way.

"It's Prue… Prue's daughter has taken an overdose. She's in hospital and Prue can't make Wednesday's performance! Who the hhhhell is…." Peter's voice trembled with worry.

"Is she alright? Good Lord!" Sheila looked up towards the ceiling as if summoning help from above.

Peter burst forth with the news. "Oh, yes, she'll be alright. But Prue's says she must stay by her side… they'll move her on to the Psychiatric Ward. She's been a headache to Prue for years… not that you'd know, bless her… Prue's normally so helpful! Two dddays to find a replacement… two bloody days… hhhow am I to do that? We can't NOT have a woman behind the counter… it's integral, it's expected, and it's all part of the full picture…. Oh, shit!"

"I don't think I could take it on as well, Peter… not now… why, I can't pour from the teapot without my hands shaking …" Sheila explained.

"Good God, no! I mean to say… of course not… I wouldn't expect… but where to look? Who the hell can I find? Veranya is away with her family in Poland… I can't call on her!"

"How nice! Your wife often goes to stay…"

"Sheila" Sheila! What AM I to *DO*???"

NOT SO PRIVATE LIVES   L TAYLOR

Eric ambled into the room. He had been putting the cups away tidily in the cupboard but not before inspecting their cleanliness and had overheard the frantic conversation in the main room.

"What's wrong now? Poor Peter, you do tend to take too much upon yourself…" he began.

Peter automatically stood up and vacated the green covered armchair to sit on a stool next to Sheila.

"Prue's out. I need another older woman to replace her… but who, where from?" Peter voice pleaded.

"Look no further, Peter, proud producer, despairing director!" Eric grinned and stood up before the other two, his hands on his hips.

"Eh?" Peter responded, rubbing his hands through his hair anxiously.

"Why, ME of course!

Sheila gasped. Peter's mouth hung open. Was he to resort to this? This, after the success that seemed so near his grasp only two nights ago, at their second performance?

"You should have seen my "Charley's Aunt" back in the 70's, eh Sheila? Eh? Why, I got as much applause as Ann did the other night, didn't I, Sheila?

NOT SO PRIVATE LIVES   L TAYLOR

You remember it, surely! I was as good as little ole **Arthur Askey… remember him? Of course in Will S's day men took female roles… it wasn't proper for women to be on stage… they had a bad reputation even then! We've a video somewhere up on the shelves here of me… Sheila's coming to mine for coffee tomorrow, morning…" Eric continued.

"Am I?" Sheila queried. She could remember being asked to help Eric do some sorting of clothes, but coffee and tomorrow? Had she agreed to that? Was her memory so bad now that she couldn't recall agreeing to that, and so soon?

"We can go over the lines for the part! I said I was always available, Peter! There! Problem solved! Stop fretting!" Eric took his coat from the rack and made ready to leave for home. He could feel excitement stirring in his stomach, always a good sign. He'd put aside the soup and maybe buy some fish and chips on his way home. Another chance to show this lot what he could still do!

Peter anxiously looked to Sheila. She took in a noticeably deep breath.

"Why, yes," she agreed, "we can always give it try, Peter?" she raised her eyebrows quizzically at him.

Peter lowered his head despondently, clasped it back between his hands and began to rock to and fro all over again. He moaned like an animal in pain.

"God, must we?" Then realising his lack of choice, he sat upright in submission "Yes, yes… I ggguess…we'll have to give it a try…."

Eric took Sheila by the elbow and steered her to the barn door.

"Come along, Sheila, my dear. Peter needs time to recover. All's well that ends well! You shall see. We old 'uns won't let you down… you can count on us!" He laughed cheerily.

As they closed the door behind them, Peter began to laugh too. He laughed and laughed and then he cried a little. Fetching a small flask hidden at the back of one of the wonkiest kitchen drawers, he soon gulped down some gin to steady his nerves before finally locking up and heading for home alone.

At Eric's Cottage

Sheila took the bus and walked the rest of the way to Eric's cottage on the outskirts of town. She had a small hold-all over her shoulder which held her personal box of make-up that she still kept, despite its lack of use now, and two copies of the play.

"Three little maids from school!
Three little maids who, all unwary
Come from a ladies' seminary
freed from its genius tutelary —"

Thus Eric sang to her on opening the cottage door. He sounded very happy and was dressed in a dazzling silk gown over shirt and trousers.

"Life is a joke that's just begun!" he sang on.

"I'm here, Eric," she stated, ignoring his singing.

He sang another verse.

"Three little maids from school are we
Pert as a school-girl well can be
filled to the brim with girlish glee
three little maids from school!"

Sheila gave him her impatient, cross look, one he had come to easily recognise over the years of knowing her.

"But dearest, we sang that at school! Surely you remember? My Boys Only and your Girls only got together for a church do…" he began and skipped boyishly ahead of her as she entered his 'front parlour', as he chose to call his living room.

Sheila took off her jacket and shoved it into his flapping hands. What did he look like? Did he think he was now the reincarnation of Coward, for goodness sake? Silly, stupid man… she had never really liked him. Sitting on the bus, she had pondered the question why then did she always help him out? A sense of true charity, perhaps, reflecting her Methodist upbringing?

He had always been arrogant, self-absorbed, selfish even and cruel. Self-deluded. Full of self-belief. Just look at him now? And offering to take the part! Goodness knows how much prompting he would need even for such a relatively small part… and the biggest fear of all, voiced by the company in his absence, was his ad-libbing… would he make free with it? Still, he could play a comic part well…. His Malvolio, from Twelfth Night, last season had been exceptional… As she had said to Peter, when he telephoned full of doubts about casting Eric in any role, what choice had they? The show must go on!

They spent time going over his lines and Eric seemed to repeat them well enough.

"Let's take a break there, Eric." Sheila suggested. She was tired and the quarrels from the flat above her had kept her awake.

"Of course, Sheila dear. I shall go over them again tonight, in front of my cheval mirror!

I can get into character then… no; leave the make - up…

I shalln't wash it off until last thing, it assists in building the character. ++Beryl Reid always did it that way- said shoes did it for her… once she put the pair on, she was into that person's character…"

"The wig fits well. Maybe less red lipstick…"Sheila leant forward as they sat together on the cushioned settle, and holding a wet wipe, attempted to wipe some lipstick from his lips..

"No, no, dear heart. They still wore bright red lipsticks in the 40's… after the dreadful war… anything to cheer themselves up. Talking of which I want to show you your next task for the day… come with me to the Caspar!" he joked.

NOT SO PRIVATE LIVES   L TAYLOR

He took the wipe from her and taking her by the arm, raised her up from the seat.

"None of your nonsense, Eric. What next?"

She followed him upstairs to his mother's bedroom and opened the old wardrobe. The musty smell mingled with the stronger smell of mothballs. Sheila looked at the old clothes hanging there. To think his late mother had urged him that once to propose to her. Sheila grinned at the memory and the pleasure she then had of turning Eric down. She knew the proposal was imminent and had let him kneel down beside her ready with the boxed ring; this exhibition had added to her pleasure in refusing him. Such arrogance he had even then! Of course he took the refusal nonchalantly and actually went on to inform her that it was his mother's idea and that she would not get such a grand offer ever again! She hadn't married it was true… but she had not lacked beaus nor offers… not that she ever confided that to the likes of Eric! Perhaps she should have done, in self defence? But it was not in her nature to fight back and cause others too much hurt.

"Well, there's some good stuff here. Marcia won't want it all, of course… she hasn't room. But other Am Drams might find some of it useful. Now this Edwardian lace collar… Marcia will love that!" she said, fingering one mourning grey dress." Hers are

NOT SO PRIVATE LIVES   L TAYLOR

so yellowed and mended from tears. People can be so careless changing costumes over. All hurry, hurry, hurry!" She turned to find Eric had left the room, left her to deal with it, talking to herself. Or were the memories too much? You could never be sure. He must have felt something when the old lady had finally passed away… grief, relief even?

She could hear him singing again from downstairs and she had to admit his voice was still good and clear for an octogenarian. She certainly couldn't match it now with years younger!

"Three little maids from school!
Three little maids who, all unwary
Come from a ladies' seminary
freed from its genius tutelary —"

Had they really performed Gilbert and Sullivan's "The Mikado" at school… all those years ago?

The Penultimate Performance

"Is he ready, then, Sheila? Is he dressed?" Peter asked anxiously as he stood at the Pavilion bar with a large glass of red wine clasped in his hand.

Sheila didn't look him in the eye. "Do stop worrying, Peter, he'll be fine!"

 Keith, the Treasurer tried to reassure him. "We've already taken enough the first two nights to cover all our costs AND we have made some profit… half way there and already a success!" He sipped at his tonic water.

Peter gulped his wine and rattled open a crisp bag. "Has he the words perfect, Sheila? Let's face it…it isn't a big part… Mrs Baggot has only the two scenes really…. Otherwise she's just pouring tea, spilling all over the cups and looking pompous. He should manage both of those!"

"He has learnt the lines and as to stage directions, I think he'll be fine… I can't answer for his ad-libbing, Peter…. Sheila lowered her voice and seemed to mumble the last of her reply-""nor his costume…" Peter's brow creased further at the thought of Eric ad-libbing only, failing to register those last mumbled words.

NOT SO PRIVATE LIVES   L TAYLOR

"He'd better not! He'd better not! "Rats" is a bit of a nightmare as it is… with my Rachel having to ad-lib to cover that daft new boy's mistakes. He keeps forgetting paragraphs of the play … keeps shifting forward to the next scene before it's been reached! I just couldn't believe it last night… the first night I put down to nerves, now I think he's just bloody hopeless at it! How the audience can follow the plot, beats me…"

John had arrived and stood at the end of the bar drinking a much earnt and needed lager, having been busy shifting scenery.

" I think most of them nod off when they see "RATS"… thank goodness, even I can recognise the gaps in dialogue… it's this sudden heat wave, makes 'em sleepier!" John chuckled.

"I just hope attendance isn't down on these next two nights… hope they don't work it so they come in just for 'Brief Encounter', not that I can blame them!" Peter commented.

 "But it won't make any difference to the takings, Pete," Keith emphasized again. "Same price tickets whatever, whichever one they come to see."

"Yes, but how does it look, eh? With the lady Mayor and her husband coming tonight, front seat! I've know Jack Smedley for years and he always

NOT SO PRIVATE LIVES   L TAYLOR

persuades her to come along… it's good publicity but that shite Alex Long is doing the article for the local rrrrag and I bet he mentions lower numbers and notices if less come in for 'RrrrATS'… it won't do our reputation much good." He drained the last of his wine from the glass noisily.

"They can't *know* which play comes first, though… because only we know that we leave the last used scenery on and do whatever that portrays next, to save time and effort…" John explained.

"Unless some smart arse has worked out our system!" Peter responded miserably.

Keith patted him on the back in a final effort to reassure him. But Peter, his head held low, like a child feeling shame, wearily ambled back to the sound system to start the incidental music cd.

The auditorium was however full as "BRIEF ENCOUNTER" began.

Eric was already on stage, standing behind the counter of the Refreshments Room as middle- aged Mrs Baggot. His wig was of grey hair held in a bun and he touched it fussily as he spoke his first words. His voice rose higher and was a little squeaky as he spoke his lines to Carey, dressed effectively as an older man, the station master.

"Oh, indeed. Very interesting, I'm sure." Eric responded to Carey's chatter. *"I'm afraid I can't stand 'ere wastin' my time in idle gossip. Time and tide wait for no man, Mr Godby"* He turned to the audience and fluttered his false eye lashes. Peter now seated next to the Mayor and her husband in the front row, grimaced but Eric had raised a titter amongst the audience and even the lady Mayor smiled a little.

"Beryl!" in character Eric called across to Sheila who had stepped on stage to act this minor part. *"Go and clean no 3! I can see the crumbs from 'ere!"* Another louder giggle was heard from the audience. Mrs Baggot now poured the tea from the Betty Brown Teapot all over the cups, nonchalantly spilling onto the tray just as directed but also humming.

But when the scene came where Albert Godby smacked Mrs Baggot on the behind as she bent down, Peter looked aghast up at the stage.

"Oooh…" Eric cried out, *"How dare you! Kindly keep your' ands to yourself!"* His expression as he turned to the audience brought loud laughter. Sheila had added more rouge to his cheeks as Eric had requested and it had certainly served its purpose. But horror of horrors! Peter could clearly see that Eric's

dress had not been fully fitted at the back and his black trousers were on show underneath!

Was this the real reason for such mirth in the audience? What could Sheila have been thinking of, or Marcia, to let him go on stage half dressed like that! He'd catch them both in the Interlude and have some words for them.

On stage, Carey responded *"When you're angry you look wonderful, just like an Avenging Angel!"*

Eric now grinned cheekily back at him and his advances. *"I'll give you Avenging Angel, takin' such liberties!"* Then unscripted, and with

Carey taking the cue of the latest ad-lib, they chased each other around the stage for a bit… Eric's costume still left open at the back… Poor Peter hung his head in shame, quietly praying to God *"please, no more!"* But the audience loved it.

A hush fell as Ann and Ian, the main characters who had fallen in love, came on stage. Ann's performance throughout was excellent. A mirror stood front left of stage and when Alec had left her to catch his train, she slowly walked over to it and stood gazing at herself to speak her thoughts.

"This misery can't last" she began, with such genuine emotion in her voice," *I must remember that. Not even life lasts very long."*

Peter observed the women in the opposite row dabbing their eyes with tissues. Wow! Geoff, standing in the aisle beside a wobbly speaker, stood mesmerized by his wife's performance.

Much to Peter's relief the lighting had dimmed at the back of the stage and Eric was standing quietly behind the counter, busy polishing glasses. Surely he too was moved by such great acting.

The last Act saw Ann yet again perform beside the mirror, as her character reflected on the end of her short, unfulfilled affair with Alec. *"No, I want to remember every minute always… always to the end of my days."*

The end of her act met with rapturous applause.

Interlude

 Backstage, Peter grabbed Sheila by the arm. She had been the Prompt aided by Marcia, both sitting at the side of the stage, out of view with Sheila dressed for her short part as Beryl.

She didn't seem surprised as he led her discreetly to back of the dressing rooms.

"His dress, his dress ISN'T DDDDONE UP! Woman, what can you be thinking of?" Peter stuttered crossly.

"Don't start on me! It would do up fine, he's skinny enough, the silly old sod of a trouper! But he said it would make him too hot… that his make-up would melt! What was I to do? You know how stubborn he is and we need him in that role…"

Peter knew she was right.

He sighed heavily and sat down on a stool left close by. "Sorry, Sheila. I understand.

 This is the last one I direct/produce… I can't take the problems anymore! That man's ego is so inflated!"

Sheila put her arms around his shoulders. She had known him and his family for years now.

NOT SO PRIVATE LIVES   L TAYLOR

"But he did some good work, Peter. He raised a laugh and more. Let him be. Anything he does that is too outrageous Ann's performance will outshine… she's simply marvellous at that part. She certainly knows how to look guilt-ridden and sorrowful; she's almost as good as Celia Johnson in the film."

"Yes, I know. Geoff puts it down to her catholic Irish upbringing… they get riddled with guilt from childhood, he reckons." Peter had calmed down.

"The show must go on, Peter!" Sheila stated, "And that bell is due soon, so off you go to your seat… Geoff is taking on the sound system for "RATS" in your place.

"God! Yes! Now we're really for it… "RATS"… bloody load of crap! That idiot even held the knife upside down last performance!" Peter shook his head despondently and left Sheila to carry on as the overworked Prompt!

Rescue

Peter put down his mobile phone. He had been playing some soothing Bach music on his new music centre when the telephone had jangled that silly tune his daughter Rachel had added to it. He sighed with relief at the news: Ian rang to say he had played that part in "RATS" some while back and Sheila had loaned him a script. He was sure he could make a better job of it than young Jason was managing even though it would be the last performance, the last night. Peter guessed he too was worried about the press report and his own standing as an actor who had chosen to participate in one of this amateur company's productions.

What a relief! He looked around his living room. Despite the deep-pile, luxurious carpet, white leather three piece, velvety curtains and matching cushions, 50 inch flat screen on the wall and all their personal knick-knacks and silver-framed photos… it didn't seem like home without his wife Veranya there.

Thank goodness, just another week and she would be home from Poland, He really needed her and her wisdom here now of course, but her family's illness was of greater concern and he certainly couldn't mention his problems in comparison to hers. It wouldn't seem fair or very caring.

Rachel was late tonight, he noticed, looking up at the ormolu clock. He had also been made aware by Prue, before her problems with her daughter had surfaced, that Rachel had been seen out in restaurants and pubs with the actor Ian. As far as he knew, Ian was still a happily married man…. So what was going on between them? Surely Rachel had not become a home-breaker, the other woman, a mistress? Modern life was full of more hazards of course and a man of Ian's age and reputation should know better. Ian was still tall, slim and good looking. That thick white hair of his, which had replaced grey so suddenly, certainly suited him well. Was that the real reason Ian had offered to take over the part in "RATS"? People could be so conniving, especially amateur actors!

Still, he ruminated, look at Ann and Geoff… who would have guessed she would take to Mike of all people. The grapevine had informed him that Mike was poorly, his drinking and overeating habits having caught up with him and now diabetes was causing him eye and leg problems

He sat back in the armchair and tried to relax with the music. He had resisted another glass of wine because since Veranya had been away, he had drunk more and eaten less He had slept in the chair two nights running now and must have nodded off when he heard the key in the front door. Should he tackle

NOT SO PRIVATE LIVES   L TAYLOR

Rachel? Was it any of his business really? She was a grown woman at 24, living back home and he liked that; her being about kept him young; she gave him some sound advice about not looking too old…. But she was already divorced once.

No, Veranya would know what to do and say, if anything... it too would have to wait for her return…

Peter sighed…Tomorrow… what further troubles were in store for tomorrow?

***

"I tell you I cannot go on… I cannot possibly perform looking like this!" Ann declared in a loud voice as she sat at her dressing table mirror.

She had developed a blood-shot eye overnight.

"Listen, Calamity Jane, it's not the end of the world! We have no stand- in for you…" Geoff told her.

"Stand- in, eh? So, your inference being that if we had…. Easy, peasy!" she replied angrily, her voice growing shriller.

"Don't start acting the Prima Donna, Nan! I won't stand for it. You know you were good, are good… I know it too! We all know it by now, damn you. I heard the audience's reaction. That's why you cannot let a little thing like this stop your final performance… probably your greatest yet!" He turned away from her and grinned to himself. Back to the old Ann then, his Ann, his Nan.

Finally persuaded, Ann arrived early at the Pavilion. Geoff went to assist John with some staging and left her in her dressing room with Sheila.

"Peter's due soon. He's suggested we either dim the lights so your red eye doesn't show… or we move the mirror over to the opposite side of the stage… it's your right eye so if we move it over then it won't be noticed."

"Humph! Good job I don't need to learn any lines, because I couldn't read them now! Goodness knows what this means… my blood pressure up again, I suppose…" Ann snapped at her.

"Or a feather caused it?" Sheila suggested.

"Feather?" *what was the daft old bat on about now, Ann wondered.*

"You could have had a feather sticking out of your pillow, poking into your eye overnight..." Sheila continued.

"Don't talk dafter than usual, Sheila! We have memory pillows, made of some man-made fibre... not old-fashioned feathers!"

Sheila ignored the rudeness of her reply. She knew Ann's temperament and all about stage fright, nerves... and Ann was no different from any other actor.

Eric waltzed into the dressing room without knocking.

"Do you mind, Eric!" I could have been undressing!" Ann snapped at him.

"I wouldn't be the first man to see you dishabille... now would I? Ha! Nor the second, nor the third!" Eric responded.

Ann continued with her makeup. "So, what do you want, Eric?

I assume you will ensure you are correctly attired this evening?" she enquired.

"That dress is too hot done up! Anyway, the audience loved it... not that your performance isn't sound, very good… some might compare it favorably with the film and the fabulous Celia Johnson… but of course you don't have her enormously sad eyes…and you cannot disguise that slight Irish twang in your voice… even in the most tender, meaningful of speeches."

Ann turned and glared at him.

"At least I don't have to prance across the stage like a demented Pantomime Dame to win applause! Carey was splendid in how he took it on so spontaneously. You're lucky to have him beside you…" Ann took up her eye drops and applied them again to her red eye. He would mention eyes!

"I'm a happily married woman, or I was…" Eric quoted cruelly from Ann's stage character.

 "Why don't you go and put on some more rouge, Eric? Spread it *all over your ugly face…* that would do nicely!" Ann took in a deep breath to calm herself down. She would not let the silly old duffer get to her; never had and never would. She'd met his sort often enough when she first began directing.

"Hahaha! Keep asking the mirror, darling… who IS the fairest of them all! Not you!

Anyway, old sour puss, good luck of course on this our final night. Bet I get more encores… or just as many anyhow…" he teased as he left, swinging his hips at the door, getting himself back into character.

The Final Performance

As the curtain rose on the scenery for "RATS" the audience grew silent. Prue's background mural of city sky scrapers and the sound of traffic filtering into the 1960's styled flat, set the scene splendidly. This play had been a lousy choice, Peter decided. He pondered on why he had chosen it in the first place, but now could think of no sensible reason why...

At the end of the one act play, thanks to Ian's professional performance, the applause was noticeably better than it had been so far. Peter sighed again, heavy with relief that "Brief Encounter" would follow and close the show. It would at least end on a good play and with Ann's performance surely win them further acclaim.

Prue was to join him in the middle row, where he had chosen to sit in order to gauge the audience reaction. He heard her arrival with the jingle of her silver bangles before she was seated.

"Sheila tells me Eric stepped in and despite ad-libbing he has done a good job." She said.

Peter turned to her and noticed the dark shadows beneath her eyes; she looked tired out. "Good to see you here, Prue. How are things?" he felt obliged to ask, although he didn't really want to hear any of her bad news, not tonight, not on this special last night… The auditorium was full and the audience hummed with anticipation. News of how good his production of "Brief Encounter" was, must have spread.

Prue took a handkerchief from the sleeve of her black sequined dress. She had managed to dress for the part, Peter noted, despite her woes.

"That skunk she took is deadly. They don't know if she will ever be right again. Just the one dose can alter the chemistry in the brain, you see. She won't be home for a very long time."

She spoke quietly and then sniffed and blew her nose rather too loudly to be ladylike.

Peter began to wonder if Prue was rather pleased to have her only daughter safely tucked away with other people to care and worry about her. Knowing how much pain Rachel's mistakes had brought himself and his beloved Veranya, he could understand why. As the music and train sounds began with the opening of the curtain on the last performance of the play, he sympathetically took Prue's hand and give it a comforting squeeze.

Eric managed a final add-lib during this last performance. As the station master, Albert, summoned by Beryl, came to protect Mrs Baggot

NOT SO PRIVATE LIVES   L TAYLOR

from two cheeky army men, during the scuffle her cakes toppled on to the floor

"Now just look at me banberries, all over the show!" Eric said, stroking his false breasts with his hands suggestively. This brought more laughter from the audience.

Peter covered his eyes with his hands as he sat with Prue. "No more! Please, God, no more! It's Charley's bloody Aunt again!" he mumbled into his lap but was unwittingly overheard by the woman sitting on the other side of him, who chuckled in response; "**he's** good isn't he? Such a sad play otherwise…"

As the final curtain fell and the applause continued, it was the players in "Rats" who came out first to take a bow. Ian especially met with a warm show of hands. But the applause didn't last long. The audience was waiting with anticipation for the players of "Brief Encounter." As tradition dictated, the lesser part players came out first, joining hands as they crossed the front of the stage and they were greeted with enthusiastic applause. Somehow Eric had managed to separate himself from them and came out as a lone figure; the audience went mad with applause and whistling.

Eric bowed perfectly, lifting off his wig and sweeping and bowing with it in his hand like a chevalier and even managed a little skip as he eventually joined the lineup.

Next onto the stage came Ann. Ian moved to her side and took her hand… the applause was rapturous now! The management gave her and also Ian, big bouquets of flowers. The rest of the cast discreetly left the stage to the two of them as they took further encores.

Standing at the sound and lights system, Geoff felt a shiver of pride at his wife. She certainly knew how to act! He had arranged an extra bouquet of flowers for her to arrive in her dressing room later.

Peter rose to his feet, clapping like a mad penguin. Keith, the treasurer stood too at the ovation, grinning from ear to ear with the thought of their overall earnings.

The press photographer's camera flashed several times and Peter had invited him back to the pavilion hall, after the audience had left, to join them at the after- show party. He hoped to get a quick look at the photos on his digital camera and hopefully an offer to read his review before it went to press, trusting that he would not linger too long on "Rats" except as a strong contrast to "Brief Encounter's" success.

Exhausted, yet exhilarated, Ann sat at her dressing table and began to remove some of her heavy makeup and wig. There was loud chatter from backstage so she hesitated, then got up to quietly close her dressing room door.

She picked up her mobile phone and dialed out.

"It went really well, Mike… yes, I miss you too… I could, yes, he's getting over it…. he won't get to know this time round…" she spoke softly, lovingly into the receiver….

Sheila took the lift up to her sixth floor flat. There was always a sense of flatness at the end of any play but this time she felt it even more. Such a success and yet it left her feeling rather low in spirit.

She looked around at her small new home; an open-plan front room which meant the kitchen could be included, thus saving space to have more occupancy and more rents coming in for the landlords. She threw off her brogue styled shoes and tiptoed over to put the kettle on. Her bedroom door and en-suite windows had been left open. She shut them, fearing a bird might fly in. One had once at her old place. She missed her old flat. It was not purpose- built like this modern one but so much bigger and airier

NOT SO PRIVATE LIVES   L TAYLOR

despite the extra cost of heating and she had a communal garden for little Trixie. Here were just lawns and no pets allowed. She missed her darling Trixie too but she had done well to live as long as she had.

She had thought of buying another dog, but a rescue one could prove problematic and a puppy would need too much early attention and she was getting too old for taking two or three walks a day and a dog must have exercise and fresh air. It would never do to keep one in here... although she had heard some odd sounds from upstairs and next door- the modern walls being so thin these day- and would hazard a guess that other tenants didn't follow the No Pets rule. Let them keep pets, why ever not? It was hard of landlords to rule them out for those lonely singles who were the most occupants here.

She made herself some chamomile tea to aid sleep and sat herself down. She had been looking at some old photo albums and they were still there, in a pile at her feet. She had too many books and albums here really... all the shelving that kind John from the am-dram company had put up for her, made the room seem smaller still... but down-sizing was hard to do at her age.

Here was a black and white one of Eric in costume… something Shakespearean but she couldn't recall the title of it just at the moment. She couldn't find one of him in a version of that old play "Charley's Aunt" though…Eric had done well yet again, pushed himself forward as ever… what an ego that man had! She was just nodding off when the telephone that hung on the wall began to ring. She went to pick it up to hear Peter's panicking voice at the other end.

"Ccccan you come bbbback, Sheila? The party is over… but oh dear, it's over in more ways than one… we need you bbbback here. Get a taxi, dear, and we can pay…."

"But Peter, what on earth…?"

He was actually crying.

"It's Eric. He went missing for the pffffer… photographer and we couldn't find him. So unlike him to be missing when there was a chance of an interview …"

"Missing? Don't upset yourself. Up to some trick again, I bet…"Poor Peter he was obviously exhausted, she decided.

Peter began sniffing loudly over the phone and it was Keith who must have taken it from him.

"Keith here, Sheila. Are you sitting down, love?" " I am now! "She said, with growing concern in her voice. " Do tell me what it is, what on earth can have happened?

"Bad news, I'm afraid. Geoff found him. Eric. He was sat on the loo. Geoff had called and knocked, thinking he had been in there too long even for Eric and his, you know, problems that he always has shared with us..."

"For goodness sake, out with it! Is he ill, taken to hospital or what?" Sheila felt her heart beating faster with a growing fear.

"Sheila, he's dead. Sorry. He died sitting there. It looks like a massive stroke to me. We've called an ambulance, oh and the police... a sudden death means questions... please can you come?"

There was a silence at the end of the telephone.

"Sheila? Sheila, are you there still? Did you hear? Can you come back please? They will want statements, you see, and you knew him best of all... poor sod." Keith said.

NOT SO PRIVATE LIVES   L TAYLOR

Sheila could feel the blood drain from her head. She must be ashen.

"Poor sod, indeed. I'll ring for a taxi soon as we put the phone down." Shattered at the news, she hung up on him.

Unsteadily, Sheila shuffled her way to the kitchen area, took out a sherry glass and bottle from the cupboard and with a shaking hand, poured herself a large drink.

"Trust you, Eric," she shouted out aloud, clutching the glass, holding it aloft as she looked upwards to her ceiling light. "Of all the ways to make an exit…. And at a peak of your performance; the final act, the best finale… one to out -do us all… you'll get more press coverage than anyone! That's just bloody typical!" She began to laugh and then the laughter grew a little hysterical and some tears began to creep from the corners of her rheumy blue eyes.

Blowing her nose, her glass lying empty on the floor beside her foot, she finally rang for a taxi to take her back to the Pavilion. Why hurry herself? He was dead! He couldn't complain about her tardiness!

When she said she couldn't really believe it, they let her see him…

NOT SO PRIVATE LIVES   L TAYLOR

Farewell (but not so fond…)

"In the midst of life we are in death
of whom may we seek for succour,
but of thee, O Lord,
who for our sins
art justly displeased?

Yet, O Lord God most holy,
O Lord most mighty,
O holy and most merciful Saviour,
deliver us not into the bitter pains of eternal death."

The coffin was lowered slowly down into the open earth as the priest read out the funeral prayer. The A.B.T.S. cast stood dressed in formal black, chosen by all out of respect for Eric's generation. The women openly wept and the men stayed brave and dry-eyed. There were two other attendants, standing further back, unknown to the gathering; they left as soon as the service had finished.

Eric's colleagues moved slowly away from the graveyard to meet again at the church hall where some refreshments had been laid on.

"What a lovely day… I mean, outside… bright blue skies, not a cloud in sight…. And the birdsong!" commented Prue, her silver bangles jangling as she took a plate and helped herself to some sandwiches and a glass of sherry.

NOT SO PRIVATE LIVES   L TAYLOR

"It was a good send-off… Sheila has taken it very bbbbadly though and has asked to talk to Keith later … apparently Eric's solicitor contacted her directly and he explained that there were ffffunds left to pay for all this… this wake or whatever…." Peter informed her.

Keith overheard and moved up the queue at the table.

"Probably Sheila has been left something in his Will then… I don't think Eric was short of a bob or two."

With their plates filled and holding their sherry glasses, Peter, Keith, Geoff, John, Ann and Prue each took hold of one of the church chairs that were stacked in a corner and soon seated themselves together in a half circle.

"Where is Sheila?" John asked concerned.

"Talking and thanking the priest, I think," Ann replied.

"She would go and see him… I never do, I always think it best to remember people as they were…" Peter said, wiping his nose and then his eyes. *Odd how funerals- and there were more and more these days to attend as one grew older- how they stirred up memories of others one had lost…Peter thought quietly to himself. Best not let any tears slip through…. Eric wasn't exactly a nice person…*

"She did see him, remember, Peter… where he was… where he died….

She told me she needed to also see him at rest, in his coffin, in order to get that ghastly last picture of him from her mind.

He was sat eyes wide open slumped back….I try not to picture it myself again, having found him there… but poor soul, she has no one else to talk to about it.." Keith explained.

Ann opened her handbag and drew out a folded newspaper.

"Read this! Even in death he manages to annoy me…" she began.

OBITUARIES

Stanley Eric Bristow   1937-2018

Eric, as he was known to his colleagues and friends, sadly passed away on Monday evening after one of his most successful acting performances that gained him several encores. He will be sadly missed by the many people who knew and worked with him.

NOT SO PRIVATE LIVES   L TAYLOR

Being a super trouper, Eric stepped in and "saved the day" when another actor was unable to perform. He bravely took on the role at short notice of Mrs Baggot from the popular 40's play "Brief Encounter" staged by A.B.T.S.

Much to the rest of the cast's distress, after his final, well received performance he suddenly collapsed offstage and died. Eric was renowned in local amateur theatre and his career as an actor, despite its amateur status, spanned several decades. His talent saw him performing to rapturous applause in a variety of roles from Shakespeare as Malvolio, (last season) through to playwrights such as Coward, Wilde and Ayckbourn.

His funeral will be on 17th May at 11a.m. and it is expected that there will be a large turn-out to say farewell to this much loved, experienced and generous performer.

"*Rapturous applause… sadly missed… super trouper*, indeed! Ann continued angrily… he was just a vicious, nasty, sarcastic, bitter, twisted…"

Geoff grabbed hold of her hands.

"Stop it, there, Nan! You'll only regret it later. And words cannot be taken back.

NOT SO PRIVATE LIVES   L TAYLOR

We know you're upset… as if he has somehow upstaged you… but he hasn't… poor sod **is** dead " he reminded her.

"I hope he rots in hell…!" she mumbled, as Geoff placed his arm around her shoulder and hugged her, trying give some comfort.

"Have you seen the local rag's review? Mention of my name was brief and not very helpful… I feel even worse reading it like that, in black and white… as if it was my fault… I let you all down!" Prue began to sob rather too loudly. Peter had noticed she was now on her third sherry.

"We're not on stage now, Prue... give over… Sheila is coming over… she'll never believe you are crying for that man!" Ann scolded her.

Prue continued to blub, holding a large man's handkerchief, possibly brought along for the sole purpose, over her face, in a feeble attempt to hide her sudden outburst of emotion.

Sheila joined them and Keith quickly gave up his seat to her and fetched a wooden stool that was left in the far corner.

"Seen this, Sheila?" Ann asked, opening the newspaper to another page, folding it back and handing it over to her.

NOT SO PRIVATE LIVES   L TAYLOR

SUCCESS & TRAGEDY STRIKE!

A.B.T.S.''s latest offering was a combination of two plays: the lesser known " RATS" murder/thriller by the Queen Of Crime, Agatha Christie and the much loved war time love story " Brief Encounter.

No one, however, could foresee the tragic, sudden demise that followed the final performance of the latter, more successful offering, of their talented and most experienced actor Eric Bristow; Eric dramatically collapsed off stage and died, of natural causes, aged 81 and yes, still acting!

His performance as a middle-aged woman, Mrs Baggot won him well deserved encores as his comical contribution to the role offset the sadness of this tragic love story. Eric, a true trouper, had apparently stepped in last thing to cover the original choice for this part, Prue Dengate who was unable to continue for personal reasons.

"RATS" without such experienced, talented participants, proved less popular until Ian Holm, an independent amateur actor of some quality, replaced the younger main character and pulled this production up by it socks!'

The staging was inspirationally created by John T….. with great effect; partitions, balconies 'magically' appeared to cover the different eras of the two sets; one example of his innovative ability was that the counter he built for the 40's play soon turned cleverly into a 60's coffee table! This show of talent should surely improve his prospects. He is worthy of more than a mere amateur company such as A.B.T.S.

Ann Summers, having to follow such memorable performances such as Celia Johnson in the film of Brief Encounter, quite shone. Her emotional expressions were truly real and her thoughts, cunningly staged as asides in a mirror, moved women in the audience to shed actual tears.

Overall this production of Peter Brown's was saved from the disastrous choice of players in "The Rats"- actors who were young and unable to work without many a noticeable prompt- by the fine comic acting of the late Eric Bristow and Ann Summer's remarkably real portrayal in the second choice of play, the ever-popular story Brief Encounter."

NOT SO PRIVATE LIVES   L TAYLOR

Sheila took the newspaper from Ann and fumbled in her handbag for her spectacles. She sat and read it as the rest of the company grew quiet, awaiting her reaction. She sighed heavily. "Well, the old codger would have loved that! You got a lovely review Ann, dear… moving the audience to tears and that was certainly true. And nice to see John T mentioned… he is talented you know… we'd be sorry to lose him, I'm sure." Her hands noticeably shaking, she folded the paper back up and returned it to Ann.

"They had to mention "Rats", of course they did, I realise that… bbbad production, bbbad casting on my part… pity it got any mention, but there you have it…" Peter scratched at his wavy hair.

"Yes, but Ian pulled it together, in the end… don't forget, Peter." Sheila added to console him.

"I just wish they hadn't put HIS so-called performance alongside mine! I'm sorry, Sheila, I realise you and he had known each other for a very long time… but it hurts… somehow he's managed to spoil it…" she began to cry now in place of Prue who had ceased her noisy blubbing as soon as the review was being read. I'll have to go… I'm sorry, everyone… I just can't stay…" Ann rose to leave.

"Go and take a long soak in the tub, love… I promised to help clear the hall for the vicar… I'll join you later." Geoff said, helping her on with her jacket.

Just before she was about to leave, Sheila stood up and faced her. "I didn't much like him, either, Ann! Wily old buggar at the best of times… but he really couldn't have foreseen his own death, dear… few of us can."

Ann nodded and managed a wry smile as she left the company.

"I wonder who those two pppeople were… the two who left before we did, to come here?" Peter queried, trying to move the subject matter on.

"Probably they just like funerals… some people attend any funeral even though they are not related… they seem to find something satisfying in them…" Keith said.

"Maybe a sense of relief because it isn't theirs yet?" Geoff chuckled lightly.

"The review in "The Theatre Today" is much better…kinder, far fairer on Ann's performance…" Keith began.

"The Theatre Today" but who could have seen to that… Peter, did you?" Geoff asked suddenly alarmed.

"No, old chap… can't say I've seen it to read it… I can't think who would have any contacts with that mag… oh, yes, MMMike did…" Peter could have bitten his tongue as the words escaped him… Geoff suddenly stood up and put his jacket on that he had left on the back of his chair.

"You off now, too?" Keith asked. He could see the sudden change in Geoff, whose body stiffened as he stood there.

"Apologise to the vicar for me, would you Keith?" Geoff asked, his facial muscles grown taut as if held in self- control…

"I need to get off home rather urgently… I need to see my wife!"

He slammed the door to as he left the church hall.

"Oh dear… "Peter exclaimed, the only one to pass comment, "oh dear…"

Outside, standing close to the heavily scented wreaths, stood John, busy on his mobile phone. His wife, Lin had missed all the action whilst away with her sister in France.

NOT SO PRIVATE LIVES   L TAYLOR

"Yes, Lin, you got my message then? Yes, *'Everyone's Aggravation'* is as dead as a dodo! Great last performance though! Pity you missed it. And it seems Ann is at it again. I know, I know," he chuckled," what are this lot like, eh? Why, you could write a book…."

The 'wake' for Eric soon broke up.

Sheila confides in Keith

"Thank you so much for coming, Keith… I didn't know who to turn to… and you and I have never had a cross word!"

Keith smiled as he entered her flat. "True, Sheila, we have had no occasion to cross words and if we had, I'm quite sure we could handle our differences with decorum and respect for one another's views. Sadly this cannot be said of other members of the Society… but actors can be 'difficult'… he took a seat as indicated beside her.

"Difficult… yes, we are… we can be… egos, it's all about egos… But to get to the point of asking for your time in coming here: I saw Eric's solicitor and in the Will he made me his sole beneficiary. I was shocked… I had no idea he would do such a thing. I realised he was all alone in the word after his mother died… but the cottage and contents seemingly are mine and a bit of money too…

"I think that's kind and generous… no one is all bad after all!"

"I've got the kettle on… or would you prefer something a little stronger? I had to myself..." she explained, twisting her hands in her laps anxiously.

"Is there something else, Sheila? Something more bothering you? Are you upset about his giving you…" Keith asked, sitting forward in his chair. He noticed a half empty large wine glass was on the side table next to her chair. This wasn't like Sheila, she seldom drank any alcohol, as far as he knew and he had visited her here before and in her last home and never seen wine about the place before now.

She picked up the glass and drank some more.

"Would you like a glass, perhaps… or was it tea, coffee?" she offered.

"Yes, I'll take a small one with you… somehow you seem to need company with it!

You stay put. I know where to find a glass."

He got up and soon found a small glass in her kitchen cupboard. Sheila had not stirred from her seat. Again this seemed out of character; she had always been fidgety and would insist on playing proper host… but this time she was too preoccupied.

Keith rejoined her and sipped a little from the glass. He preferred spirits, when he did partake, but was too polite to remark on this and doubted if Sheila had anything like that to suit.

"It wasn't just about the Will… I've had a phone call and the cottage was broken into yesterday… she began.

"Heavens above, no! We none of us thought to see if his home and stuff were secure… too much else going on… and of course, as you rightly pointed out, he has no one else.. These burglars sometimes get news of coming funerals… and make a kill, so to speak…"

"Oh, it's okay. The police found out about me from the solicitor and I went around. I have never been in the place alone… he always kept it so spick and span… such a fussy old devil… it was probably some local kids who broke in…. Probably he had upset them, he was good at upsetting people, I won't deny, not even now he's dead… and one shouldn't talk ill and all that… They smashed some vases and ornaments he kept on the window sills, ransacked the cupboards… nothing much taken; he never left money in the house as far as I know… His bedroom had been well searched…. Under the mattress, ripped with a knife … oh and his late mother's bedroom… No, it was what I found. Pages ripped from his diaries." She finished the last of her wine.

"Diaries? Yes, I can imagine he would keep a diary… plenty of spare time to do so…"

NOT SO PRIVATE LIVES   L TAYLOR

"They went back decades, Keith... and the burglars had ...well, how to say it... peed on most of them!"

"The little... so and so's... I hope the police get the little swines..." Keith stated.

"I put them in a plastic bag... what was left, not torn up or too wet and smelly...what I could still read... some of it was handwritten in the earlier years and I never could read his spidery scrawl... What is it they say? Small writing means a small mind? It seems he didn't write so often later on...when he took to typing, unless some have been actually taken away... he didn't make entries every day as before. I want to show you just one sheet... I shall probably burn the rest..." She produced a file that had lain beside her on the settee unnoticed.

"What about prints?" Keith suddenly thought to ask.

" They must have had the foresight to wear gloves... the police couldn't find any prints... well, only the one set and they turned out to be his... same as the ones on the tablet bottle beside his bed, you see...

 He was always so fussy, cleaning and polishing. Open it and read Keith, please." Keith sat back in his chair and read the two sheets of typed paper.........

Feb 17 2018   despite her toffee-nosed airs, Ann has proved herself to be a trollop like most women of her age…. Sexual freedom they call it! Fancy her and that arrogant little shit, Mike P having it off together. Talk about two rabid dogs on heat!

March 9 2018…. Brown has had to replace that dippy creature PRUE with me as Mrs Baggot. What does she think she looks like, dressed in such passion- killing long skirts and jangling away like some mangy feline desperate for a quickie in some long grass!

I shall show them a thing or two about acting! That Peter as a producer- just an over-paid, over-pensioned typical Civil Service Manager- has about as much ability to do the job as a worm would have trying to take flight!

March 2 2018   Have persuaded the rather gullible but kindly Sheila to help sort Mama's clothes. A task I just cannot bring myself to accomplish. She's made of tougher stuff than me. I sometimes wish she had agreed to marry me when I asked her all those years ago (see diary 1967) but my pride would never allow me to ask her again. Anyway, I don't think she has feelings for me however hard I have tried to encourage some warmth betwixt us. Most women have left me cold, thanks to that overbearing bitch of a mother of mine (God forgive me!) but Sheila, ah, there's

NOT SO PRIVATE LIVES   L TAYLOR

the rub, I could have learnt how to love with her, I know that now, late in my life, too late in my life.... I think I have always known she could be the only choice for me.

April 11 2018- had some awful dreams about Mama. Maybe removing the last vestige of her, namely her clothes, her scent..... I'm changing my Will. She always said no one would suit me or could be good enough....

Scoffed at the idea of me and S.... I'll show her... BITCH! BITCH! You BITCH up in heaven or hell! Wish you had died sooner and released me...too late, all too late of course. Thankful for this part in B.E. ...my life without acting? Impossible! It's the balm, pain barrier...lost, lost in another time, inside another personality.

"Oh, dear... not very nice!" Keith commented, putting the file down on the coffee table." But not too surprising. That was Eric..."

"He took to typing on his Olivetti otherwise I wouldn't have managed to read what I did.... But this sheet bothered me. Wily old devil, I do believe he hoped I would find the typed stuff. Look at the date... Changing his Will in April... what rubbish! The solicitor told me his Will was written and changed three years ago! I was meant to find this... I was meant to feel bad because I turned him down!" Tears could be seen coursing down her cheeks.

"Sheila.... He sounds here as if he was very fond of you... but the rest is pretty bitchy, isn't it... were other entries as bad?"

Sheila mopped her eyes with a tissue. "Oh, yes... you heard what the late *Kenneth Williams wrote in his diaries about the people he had met... well, Eric's comments, those left readable, were just as nasty!

"So... why so upset? You weren't obliged to accept him. "Keith commented, confused by her show of emotion. Perhaps the wine had added to her feeling so unhappy. It could act as a depressant, especially at such times.

 "I never loved him. I never could love him!"

"Then that's alright... you had your own feelings and were entitled to them, surely."

"But I didn't realise how much damage she had done him, you understand..."

Keith frowned, still not yet comprehending the cause of her distress.

NOT SO PRIVATE LIVES   L TAYLOR

"I only met her twice, never again after she was bed-ridden. She had him running around for her but then that happens to men who don't leave their mothers…"

Keith nodded and sipped the rest of the wine in his glass. He said nothing and wisely let her talk it all out.

"His father died in a P.O.W. Camp during the last war… he had a photo of him but he never knew him. He was quite high up in the military. But he hinted, you see, he often hinted how **she,** his mother, was. Boarding school he hated. Boys were beaten as part of their so-called education in those days and he actually mentioned his beatings… only that he had had them not any description…. And he'd grin and then comment that it didn't do him any harm and how it should be brought back into the school curriculum….I never reacted as such, except in realising he was damaged and not the one for me! But to write 'bitch'' about her…his own mother and to hope she was in hell? God above, what must the man have suffered under her to turn like that?"

She started to visibly shake. Keith now got up and sat beside her. He took her cold, wrinkled hands in his and held them tightly.

"Sheila, dear, kind lady, none of this was your fault or of your doing…"

"But I knew… I guessed he was damaged… he writes here…" she took up the file and opened it to the relevant page… "*I could have learnt how to love with her*…I let him down. I should have said something and made him open up… cared more..."

"Why? Why should you? You didn't love him, you just said so!" Keith placed her hands on her lap. Why is it you women always think it's your job to change us, save us from ourselves!"

She looked more thoughtful and had calmed down now.

"But… no one loved him… everyone deserves some love from someone surely… their parents, I mean…"

"It is tragic, I agree. But I think he wrote that because he was feeling depressed about his life… he could have pursued you further if he did love you so much… if he truly believed you, or come to that, anyone without some kind of specialist training, could help him to heal…but he didn't, did he? He didn't ask you again… he kept all his hurt and bitterness and spurted it out on other people... turned to acting it out as well and that is how he managed to live as long as he did, I think. True love finds a way… I've heard you say that often."

Sheila nodded in agreement.

"Burn these pages, Sheila… along with the rest and take his cottage… he wanted you to have it… that way you **are** giving him something he wanted!"

"Yes. Yes… I would like the cottage. He knew I wasn't that happy moved here, too small and no pets allowed. It has two bedrooms too and I might have a couple of kittens… not another dog, though… cats can look after themselves. I admired the garden and I'd keep that the same... my grandniece is looking for somewhere to lodge… she's won at place at the local Uni… did I tell you about her?" her mood had lifted along with her sense of guilt.

She had told him about her niece but Keith encouraged her nevertheless. "No, go on."

"I'll put the kettle on for some coffee, shall I?" she suggested, standing up and straightening her skirt.

"What a good idea. And Sheila..." he said, taking out the diary pages…" tear these up?"

She took them and standing in front of him, just managing a smile, she tore them up into pieces.

NOT SO PRIVATE LIVES   L TAYLOR

Whatever next?

The A.B.T.S. *B.A.T.S.* met on a fine September evening, to discuss which play to choose next.

All were in attendance and on time. Ann couldn't resist remarking that it must be a first.

Geoff had been very solemn and moody with her of late. It all stemmed from the time he had found out about Mike's review of her performance in "Brief Encounter" and written it up in that wretched magazine "The Theatre Today". Ann had tried hard to convince him that she had not seen Mike again and that she was just as mystified as he was as to how or why he had written such an article on her behalf. She claimed she was not aware that he had ever been to see the play but this was met with more upset; Geoff actually shouted at her that he wondered how Mike would be allowed to write a review, if he had not known something about it!

Now every time she went out without him, Geoff had taken to constantly asking her where she was going, who she was seeing there and how long before her return.

"He's driving me mad, Prue! I do love him but I wish he would stop this watching over me all the time… everything I do, everywhere I go, he's asking

NOT SO PRIVATE LIVES   L TAYLOR

why, who, when. It's bordering on paranoia!" She sipped at her coffee.

"He must get over it, same as my Cynthia!"

"Same? I fail to see how it's the same as Cynthia? How is she doing, by the way?" Ann asked, trying to hide her annoyance at her likening the two. Prue's main talent lay in creating gossip.

"Well, she came to stay once or twice when they let her out of the funny bin…"

Ann winced at Prue's description of her daughter's stay on a Psychiatric Ward due to an overdose.

"We never did get on, Cyn and I… she must get over it or not… it's her problem after all. Same as Geoff's suspicions are down to Geoff, aren't they? She's moved back to that ghastly high rise flat in Camden and has another new boyfriend… I just hope he's a better influence, than the last one. I dunno, you give them all the freedom and you get no thanks for it… hold them back and you are possessive, being over-protective; let them go and you obviously don't care. I can't win with that daughter of mine. Must be like her father… not that I can remember much about him! I had to fight for my freedom, Ann, I left home and moved into a Commune… the last of its kind, sadly… and I was only just into my teens then…

NOT SO PRIVATE LIVES   L TAYLOR

Oh, happy days!" she sighed and twiddled with her silver bangles. Ann noticed she had extra silver rings on today- big, ugly looking things and on every finger.

"Susie's doing well. She brings her washing home and takes a few meals with us still, which Geoff moans about… but she still needs support.

She's still so young. Ah, here comes Sheila with her plate of cakes… she bought them this time…."

"Another cake, ladies?" Sheila smiled down at the two sitting so closely together and wondered what they had been discussing. Everyone had noticed the change in Ann and Geoff's relationship. She had been emboldened to comment to Ann that trust was a precious thing and once lost, hard to regain, but she didn't think Ann was too pleased with that opinion as at the time she had quickly changed the subject.

"Lovely, Sheila dear! Not as wholesome I don't suppose as home baked, but nevertheless greatly appreciated!" Prue took two more cakes and had soon eaten them, sucking the sticky icing on the top of them from her long, bejeweled fingers.

Ann decided to 'mingle' with the others, finding Prue's manners at times too low class for good company.

NOT SO PRIVATE LIVES   L TAYLOR

"Are you settling down, okay, now Sheila?" Keith asked, taking the empty cake plate from her and offering her another sherry.

"I won't take another, thank you, Keith. One is quite sufficient. Yes, my niece is moving in soon and my new kitchen is coming along nicely... Eric's must have dated back to the 60's... nothing fitted which traps dirt of course... and the cooker, scrubbed clean enough, but so outdated. I much prefer clean electric to gas anyway."

"What did you do about the furniture there... you had your own at the flat?" Keith continued.

"Oh, yes. Carey and his mate helped move me! He's such a kind, sweet young man... Mike should be proud of him. I told them they could take anything that had been moved into the garden and sell it or keep it... they seemed pleased.... Some of it was probably antique... but they deserved it. Do you know, young Carey came back with a wad of notes for me from the sale?"

Keith smiled.

"I didn't take it. Keep it or give it to the homeless, whatever, I told him. Anyway, my stuff fitted fine and has helped me to settle. I might repaper later on.

I've got my two new kittens, black and white, brothers… apparently people don't like black and white cats… can you believe that? Whatever is wrong with black and white cats?" she queried.

"Whatever is wrong with people, more like?" Keith replied.

Sheila took his hand in hers. " You were a great help, Keith… you know that…?" she let his hand go.

"Ah, we are summoned! Come on Sheila-to the table and the inevitable argument…"

"I think there will be less of that now… now Eric has passed on." she said, taking the chair he had drawn out for her.

"Less fun!" he whispered mischievously into her ear. Sheila giggled out loud.

"Take more water with it, Sheila!" Peter teased, sitting at the top of the table and calling down to her. Everyone laughed kindly.

 "Carey is writing his first play…" Marcia stated. She had to find some way of entering their conversation as, being just wardrobe lady, they left her out too often.

NOT SO PRIVATE LIVES   L TAYLOR

Carey was seen to blush. Why was it women could never keep a secret?

"Oh, yes and what will it be about?" Peter asked cheerily and without a stutter.

"It's about an old actor… a bit of a tyrant really… 'The Man Who Couldn't Stop Acting' is the title…" He looked towards Sheila and they both grinned at each other." Sheila is helping me fill out some background…."

"That sounds interesting! Why, young man, we might end up ppperforming that!" Peter spoke lightly. Veranya was back at home of course and life seemed worth all the hassle. She had persuaded him to take the Chair and to go on producing. She said he would be lost without it. Naturally, he had responded that he was lost without her!

"Moving on…." Ann interrupted… "What shall it be this time; something light and entertaining perhaps for a change … to bring in more family… with a bit of music?" She suggested, looking directly at Peter for some support.

"We don't want anything too complicated or with much scenery and props… not now we've lost John T! We'll need to make do more with costume alone…" Keith warned.

NOT SO PRIVATE LIVES   L TAYLOR

"What about the Mikado then?" Carey asked.

For once in perfect unison all the others responded loudly and as a chorus with just two words…
"OH… NO!!!

At this, Sheila sat back in her chair and, much to everyone else's bewilderment, began laughing and laughing and laughing….Would she never stop?

Also by L Taylor - in paperback from www.lulupress.com www.amazon.co.uk www.goodreads.com

"DANGEROUS DOLLS" ... follow up- "MURDER UNMASKED"

"TALES OF TWO GINGER TABBY CATS" also available in large print

"MOLLIE + CO"- follow up- "MOLLIE ALONE"

"TO GULLS ' REST".   "SECRETS & SORROWS".

"13 STRANGE STORIES." followed by "EXTRAORDINARY STORIES." "EXTRAORDINARY STORIES & OTHERS"

"THE MUST READ MEDLEY COLLECTION OF SHORT STORIES (25)"

"SISTERHOOD". "TELLING DREAMS".

"JACK." "JUST THREE GIRLS".

"OUR BREAD AND BUTTER".

"WHO PUT THE DOGS OUT, PLAYERS AT PLAY, FAT."

"NOT SO PRIVATE LIVES." "MEMORIES & MEMOIRES" "THE RESPONSIBLE CHILD"

"ON GOING BACK" "IN HER IMAGE"

"THE SPECIAL FRIENDSHIP OF SASSY & JIMMY"

"NO MORE THROUGH A GLASS DARKLY"

"TO LOVE OR NOT TO LOVE"

"BEHIND THE SHOP COUNTER"

www.amazon.com/author/ltaylorscribere

NOT SO PRIVATE LIVES   L TAYLOR

Recommended reading- RATS –Agatha Christie

Brief Encounter- Noel Coward play and film.

* **Kenneth Charles Williams** (22 February 1926 – 15 April 1988) was an English actor, best known for his comedy roles and in later life as a raconteur and diarist. He was one of the main ensemble in 26 of the 31 _Carry On_ films, and appeared in many British television programmes and radio comedies, including series with Tony Hancock and Kenneth Horne.[1][2]

 ****Arthur Bowden Askey**, CBE (6 June 1900 – 16 November 1982) was an English comedian and actor. Askey's humour owed much to the playfulness of the characters he portrayed, his improvisation, and his use of catchphrases, which included "Hello playmates!", "I thank you" (pronounced "Ay-Thang-Yaw"), and "Before your very eyes".

++**Beryl Elizabeth Reid**, OBE **(17 June 1919 – 13 October 1996) was a British character actress of stage and screen. She won the 1967 Tony Award for Best Actress in a Play for _The Killing of Sister George_, the 1980 Olivier Award for Best Comedy Performance for _Born in the Gardens_, and the 1982 BAFTA TV Award for Best Actress for _Smiley's People_. Her film appearances included _The Belles of St. Trinian's_ (1954),**

CONTD:

The Killing of Sister George (1968), *The Assassination Bureau* (1969) and *No Sex Please, We're British* (1973).

+++*Charley's Aunt* is a farce in three acts written by Brandon Thomas. It broke all historic records for plays of any kind, with an original London run of 1,466 performances.

The play was first performed at the Theatre Royal, Bury St Edmunds in February 1892. It was produced by former D'Oyly Carte Opera Company actor W. S. Penley, a friend of Thomas, who appeared in the principal role

Printed in Poland
by Amazon Fulfillment
Poland Sp. z o.o., Wrocław

63246021R00082